Praise for Danielle Devour

'I don't know what to rate this book at ... The spicy scenes are alright but the end made me feel some kinda way.'
*Bigfoot Threw Rocks at Me (So I F*cked It) – Goodreads Review*

***

'Emily SUCKS ... She forgets their anniversary and runs off to hang out in the woods and track bigfoots, there's some smut and she ends up sleeping with the alpha ... and then they all have a super fun orgy in the woods. Yikes.'
*Bigfoot Threw Rocks at Me (So I F*cked It) – Goodreads Review*

***

'i've now read TWO big foot books. wtf is wrong with me'
*Bigfoot Threw Rocks at Me (So I F*cked It) – Goodreads Review*

***

'When I started this story, I did not know what to expect. It was truly an experience that surprised me. It has a good storyline with plenty of action and drama.'
*Bigfoot Threw Rocks at Me (So I F*cked It) – Amazon Review*

About the Author

DANIELLE DEVOUR loves two things in this life: folklore and HP Lovecraft. After working for years as a ghostwriter, penning romance under the names of others, she decided to do it for herself. What transpired was a mash-up of spice, horror, and weird fiction.

Also by Danielle Devour

*Bigfoot Threw Rocks at Me (So I F*cked It)*
*Mothman Wrecked My Car (So I F*cked Him)*

MOTHMAN
WRECKED MY CAR
(SO I F*CKED HIM)

DANIELLE DEVOUR

veil and
vortex

For those who enjoy anal play and dubious consent.

Chapter One

It's Friday night and while all my friends are out having a good time, I'm sitting at the bar of the Point Pleasant Cosplay Convention hoping to get laid by a man dressed as Mothman.

I apologize for throwing you into the story like this but we don't have time for pleasantries. I'm on a mission. A mission to get fucked by my all-time favorite cryptid.

I swivel around on my bar stool and survey the scene. All around me are nerds dressed up to the nines as their favorite characters (I mean that lovingly. There's nothing wrong with a good nerd. Hell, I'm obsessed with Mothman, you think I'm *not* a nerd?).

I order a drink from the bar. Then a second. A third quickly follows, but there's still no sign of the Mothman cosplayer. Maybe I've missed him. Maybe he's already gone back to the hotel.

I first saw him earlier today, when I was at work. The Point Pleasant Hotel was overrun with cosplayers checking in for the weekend. I spent my entire shift handing out keycards and answering questions about Wi-Fi passwords, all the while surrounded by anime characters, and Marvel rip-offs. It was chaos, but I didn't mind. It made the day go faster.

Just as my shift was ending, I saw him. The elevator doors slid open, and out walked Mothman. Full costume. Glowing red eyes. Feathery antennae. The whole deal. He (or maybe she, or they) was headed for the exit. I didn't see their face. Didn't even hear them speak. But inside, I knew this was my chance.

I've been obsessed with Mothman since I was a kid. I've read every book, watched every documentary, and fallen down every conspiracy theory rabbit hole. There's something about him – the mystery, the danger, the way he's always watching but never seen. It's intoxicating. And now, here he is. Well, here's someone dressed as him. It's as close as I'm ever going to get to the real thing.

So I sit here, nursing my fourth drink, and scanning the room for any sign of those iconic wings. The bar is packed with cosplayers, but none of them are *him*.

Come on, Mothman. Don't leave me hanging.

Just when I'm about to give up, I see him. My knight in pleather armor. He's standing near the edge of the room, those glowing red eyes scanning the crowd like he's searching for something – or someone. Maybe me. Probably not. But a girl can dream.

I stand up, more than a little tipsy, and make my way over. My steps are steady, but my confidence feels like it's held together by sheer willpower and vodka. When I reach him, I lean against the wall, trying to look casual.

"Hey," I say, flashing what I hope is a charming smile. "Great costume. You really nailed the whole 'ominous, sexy cryptid' vibe".

The cosplayer tilts his head. He doesn't say anything, just stares at me with those red, rubbery eyes. It should be creepy, but somehow it's... kind of hot?

I press on. "So, uh, I'll be honest with you. I've got a thing for Mothman. Like, a *big* thing. Ever since I was a kid. I mean, who wouldn't love a guy with wings, right?" I laugh nervously, then immediately regret it. Smooth, Sarah. Real smooth.

Still, he doesn't speak. Just keeps staring.

"Anyway," I continue, lowering my voice, "I was wondering if you'd be up for... I don't know, helping me live out a weird little fantasy tonight? No pressure, obviously. But if you're into it, I know a place."

What am I doing? I'm not usually this bold. But there's something about the way he's looking at me – like he's actually considering it – that makes me feel like maybe, just maybe, this isn't the worst idea I've ever had.

The cosplayer nods and motions to the exit. Without another word, we head out to the parking lot. I'm fishing for my keys when he lays his hand on my forearm, shaking his head.

"You're right, I probably shouldn't drive. I've had a few to drink. You got a car?"

He nods again. God, this stoic act is hot. If he keeps this up, I'll have cum three times over just from the car ride.

The mysterious cosplayer leads me to his car, a beat-up sedan that looks like it's seen better days. He opens the passenger door for me, a surprisingly chivalrous gesture, and I climb in. He walks around to the driver's side, his wings brushing against the side of the car as he moves. When he opens the door, he pauses, lifting his hands to his head like he's about to remove the mask. My heart skips a beat.

"Don't," I blurt out, louder than I mean to. He freezes, those rubbery eyes locking onto mine. "Leave it on," I add, softer this time. "Please."

He hesitates for a moment, then lowers his hands. With some effort, he folds himself into the driver's seat, his wings crammed awkwardly against the roof and door. The car groans under the strain, and I can't help but laugh.

"It's not far," I reassure him, buckling my seatbelt. "I'll lead the way."

We drive in almost complete silence, with me giving directions on where to turn. The only sound is the tires on the road, the car indicator blinking, and the sound of me shuffling uncomfortably against the car seat. I'm wet already. Every bump in the road threatens to have me spill over before we can get there. I breathe deeply, trying to calm myself. This could be my one and only chance to play out my Mothman fantasy. I don't want to fuck it up.

After a short drive, we arrive at the McClintic Wildlife Management Area. The place is eerie at night, all sprawling shadows and the occasional glint of moonlight on water. It's quiet, too –

the kind of quiet that makes you feel like you're being watched. Which, given the history of this place, isn't exactly surprising...

The McClintic WMA is huge – over 3,600 acres of farmland, woodlands, and wetlands dotted with ponds. During the day, it's a peaceful spot for hiking and birdwatching. But at night? It's something else entirely. Back in the late '60s, this was ground zero for Mothman sightings. People claimed to see a winged creature with glowing red eyes lurking around here, and the stories only got weirder from there. Some said he was a harbinger of doom. Others thought he was just a misunderstood cryptid trying to mind his own business. Either way, this place is basically Mothman's hometown.

And now here I am, bringing a guy in a Mothman costume to the one spot on Earth where the real thing might actually show up. I've sobered up enough to realize how insane this is. Sobered up enough to say no and turn back if I wanted to.

But I don't want to. I want to see this through.

"Follow me," I whisper into the black mask, my breath fogging against the PVC, "I know a secluded spot where no one will see us. We can fuck to our heart's content."

I take the cosplayer's hand and lead him through the winding paths of the nature reserve. We reach a small clearing where the trees are dense around us.

The cosplayer and I stand facing one another. The moonlight filters through the canopy above, casting an eerie glow over the forest floor. Crickets chirp in the distance, their melody an unwitting soundtrack to what's about to occur. My heart hammers against my chest, the thought of finally getting what I've desired for so long making me weak at the knees.

My mystery lover stands motionless, waiting for me to make the first move. I circle him like a predator, admiring every bulge and contour of his costume. It's not the most realistic costume, and it's a little ill-fitting if I'm honest. But in the dimness of the night, and with a little imagination, I can pretend he's the real deal.

I take a deep breath and step towards him.

"Oh, Mothman," I say, my voice trembling. "I've waited my whole life for this moment. I never thought you'd actually come to me." The cosplayer remains silent, but inclines his head slightly. Emboldened, I reach out and caress the soft fuzz of his costumed chest. "Ever since I was a little girl I dreamed of you visiting me. I used to leave my window open at night, hoping you'd fly in and take me away on an adventure."

My hands trail over the firm curves of his biceps. To my disappointment, I realize they are foam padding and not actual muscle. The guy underneath is obviously not as built as I was hoping...

"All the other girls had crushes on pop stars and athletes, but you were the only one for me. No one else understands like you do. I've never wanted anyone or anything more than I want you right now."

There's a pause, and then a muffled voice comes from inside the mask.

"Should... Should I speak? I'm not sure if Mothman can talk or not."

I blink, confused for a moment.

"No. Mothman doesn't speak," I say, a little sharper than intended. I force a smile, mentally resetting myself, then jumping back into the roleplay. "Your wings are so-"

"My name's Steve, by the way."

Ew. No. I don't want to know his name is Steve. Steve isn't sexy. Steve isn't Mothman.

"Sssh," I whisper, pressing my finger hard against the mouth of the mask. "No more talking. You're Mothman now."

He nods, seeming to understand. I decide to dive ahead a bit, hoping this will get us back on track.

"Let me taste you, Mothman," I breathe, dropping to my knees in front of him, "I've waited so long for this."

Slowly, pretend-Mothman reaches down and places a gloved hand on my head, gently guiding me toward his crotch. My fingers tremble as I undo the zip, revealing his hard... Well, actually, it's not *that* hard. More of a semi. It appears Steve takes a second to get warmed up.

"Oh my god," I say, doing my best impression of a woman who's just seen the biggest cock of her life. My acting has obviously worked as his cock expands and hardens in front of my eyes. It's a respectable size. Nothing to write home about. It's exactly what I'd expect from a man called Steve, if I'm honest.

I take a deep breath and try to refocus my thoughts.

"Mothman, what a big, juicy cock you have. It's so…" I struggle to think of a word to describe the mild disappointment in front of me. "…thick?"

Gingerly, I wrap my fingers around his shaft. His cock twitches in my grip, growing harder by the second.

Ok, ok, this is good. I can work with this.

"Fuck, that feels good," he rasps through his mask.

"Steve. Don't speak," I say, "please?"

I run my fingers along his shaft, feeling the warmth and the firmness of him. He moans, and I feel a throb between my legs. This is really happening!

I lean in and take him into my mouth. His cock is salty – the cock of a human man – but in my mind I'm really sucking Mothman's dick. I moan around his girth, savoring the feel of him in my mouth.

His hand tightens in my hair, gently guiding me, urging me to take more of him. I oblige, sliding him deeper, my tongue swirling around his shaft. He tastes like sweat and latex. I should have thought about this. That costume must be hella sweaty. Maybe I've got some wet wipes in my bag…

He reaches down and caresses my breasts through my sweater. I moan, momentarily forgetting the wet wipes, pushing my chest into my hand. He kneads my breast, squeezing it roughly. It reminds me of my first boyfriend; the lack of experience and eagerness. What was his name? God, it wasn't 'Steve' was it?

I shake my head, trying to rattle the thoughts away. If only he hadn't spoken and told me his name was fucking Steve.

I've been stroking and sucking his cock for a while now and I can tell he's getting pretty aroused. At least one of us is having a good time...

Slowly, I pull away from his cock, my chin shiny with my own saliva. Steve – I mean Mothman – grunts, an urgency in his tone that wasn't there before. I grab his hand and gently pull him to the ground.

Slowly, I hitch up my skirt and peel off my panties. My pretend-Mothman growls approvingly. Playfully I throw my panties at him, expecting him to catch them, but the mask must be clouding his vision because he doesn't even try to catch them and they land on one of his pipe-cleaner antennae.

"Sorry, let me just..." I say awkwardly, reaching out to retrieve them and throw them aside.

I lie back, propping myself up on my elbows. Reaching down, I trace my fingers along my slit. I slide two fingers inside, pumping them slowly, getting myself nice and wet. My back arches and a moan escapes my lips.

Pretend-Mothman positions himself between my thighs, the head of his cock nudging my entrance.

"Fuck me, Mothman, make me yours!" I beg. But when Steve tries to penetrate me, he misses, poking my ass cheek instead. His mask slips forward, and I catch it before it fully falls off his head.

"Sorry," he mumbles, pushing his mask back on, "I can't really see shit in here."

I sit up and rub the bridge of my nose with my fingers, exasperated.

"It's ok," I say, although it really isn't. "I'll go on top."

With a sigh of resignation, I straddle pretend-Mothman, positioning myself over his dick. I take a deep breath, willing myself to get into the moment. I remind myself that this is Mothman, my childhood crush, and not a random overly enthusiastic cosplayer named Steve.

I lower myself down onto him, feeling his girth fill me up. It's... not bad, I guess.

I start to grind my hips against him, trying to find some sort of rhythm that will bring me closer to the edge. I close my eyes, imagining Mothman's powerful arms around me, his wings surrounding us like a sexy, leathery taco. But no matter how hard I try, I can't seem to get into it.

I pause my grinding and look down at pretend-Mothman. His rubbery eyes stare blankly up at the sky, his pipe cleaner antennae droop sadly to the side. Well, that's the last of my arousal draining away...

"This isn't really working for me," I admit. "Let's switch this up," I say, getting on my hands and knees.

Pretend-Mothman eagerly positions himself behind me, his hands gripping my hips. I glance back over my shoulder and see his (almost) muscular form behind me. Yeah, this could work. I haven't got a great view of him, but that could work in my favor.

I can see just enough to get me hot without his costume ruining the effect.

Steve guides himself to my entrance and pushes inside me. I think back to all the smutty Mothman fan-fic I've read, trying to place myself in the position of the helpless, horny protagonist. Steve picks up the pace, and the sound of his costume smacking against the back of my thighs starts to do something for me.

"Yes, fuck me, Mothman. Dominate me like I'm your naughty little prey," I beg.

A strange sound echoes through the darkness, making us both freeze. It's an odd chittering sound, not like anything I usually hear when I visit the nature reserve. I turn to look back at Steve who's pulled out, his head whipping around, scanning the shadowy trees surrounding us.

"Just ignore it, Steve," I say, my tone tinged with annoyance.

He enters me again and I let out an involuntary moan, but the chittering comes again. Steve hesitates, his body tense.

"Steve," I whisper urgently. "Just fuck me. It's probably a squirrel or something."

Reluctantly, Steve resumes, but his thrusts have lost their previous intensity.

"I'm sorry, but I don't think it's a squirrel," he whispers through the mask.

"Steve, seriously, can you just-"

Before I can finish my sentence, the sound comes again, louder, sending goosebumps down my spine. It was closer too, much closer. Closer than I'd like.

"Steve, what the fuck is that?" I whisper, my voice shaking.

The unnerving chittering grows louder, its frenzied rhythm pounding in my ears like a tribal drum. Steve trembles behind me, his body paralyzed with terror as we both wait for whatever is lurking in the shadows to reveal itself.

Suddenly, a loud swooshing fills the air and a heavy thud shakes the ground. I squeeze my eyelids together, refusing to bear witness to the terror that lurks so close by. Steve's hands, previously gripping my thighs, begin to slide off me. He holds me tighter, his gloved fingers clawing into the flesh of my hips as he's torn from me. But still, I don't open my eyes. If I don't see it, it can't hurt me. But the blood-curdling screams and gurgles that escape from Steve's mouth before falling silent confirm that whatever is out there, probably doesn't care if you can see it or not.

Frozen in a state of primal fear, pussy and ass exposed, I strain my ears for any sign of life. Any sign that Steve is still there. But the only sound that breaks through the deafening silence is the beating of my own heart.

Palms sweating and heart pounding, I open my eyes and roll over onto my back. As I lie on the forest floor, my eyes adjusting to the darkness, I see it. Not Steve's body, but something else... Looming above me, bathed in the faint glow of the moonlight, is a surreal and terrifying creature. Its muscular body is akin to a colossal statue, sculpted with intricate precision, covered in tufts of dark fur that shimmer under the night sky. Towering wings, reminiscent of a moths, unfolded behind it. The texture is like ancient, weathered parchment. Atop its head, two large, curved antennae protrude, twitching in the cool air. The creature's eyes, large and unblinking, are deep pools of crimson. It stands at my feet, looking down on me; a blend of beauty and menace, a guardian of the night. And there, between its legs, protrudes the most majestic cock I have ever seen.

Chapter Two

Mothman, the real Mothman, looks down at me, his eyes boring into mine. I feel his gaze burning into me, seeming to pierce my very soul. His eyes glow an unearthly red, like twin coals smoldering in the darkness. He stands over me, his massive wings spread wide, shadowing my trembling form. I want to look away, but I'm transfixed, caught in his hypnotic stare. It's as if he can see straight into my soul, see all the naughty fantasies I've been hiding my whole life.

His eyes drift down to my half-naked body. My breasts are exposed, spilling over the top of my bra. My legs are spread apart, my pussy glistening with arousal. I feel my core twitch as his eyes fix on my most private area. He seems to contemplate me for a moment as I lie here, panting, transfixed by the sight of the creature that has haunted my dreams for so long.

As he stares, unmoving, I allow my own gaze to roam over his form. His body is the perfect fusion of man and insect, rippling with raw, primal power. His chest is a bastion of muscle, each ripple and shadow dancing in the moonlight. His shoulders, broad and powerful, easily support the majestic wings that stretch from his back.

I allow my eyes to drop lower, taking in the sight of his bulging lower half. My breath catches in my throat at the sight of it. His shaft is as long and thick as my forearm, but it's not made from skin. It's translucent gold, like a hardened amber from a tree. It twists to form a corkscrew ending with a bulbous tip. With each beat of his rapid heart, it throbs slightly. I watch, horrified and aroused as a drop of clear, viscous fluid oozes from the tip and lands on the forest floor, hissing as it comes into contact with the moist earth.

Mothman's gaze rises from my dripping folds and meets my own once more. Against my better judgment, against everything I know to be good and pure and true, I want him. He is everything I have dreamed of, everything I have ever wanted and desired.

I bite my lower lip, unable to tear my eyes away from his throbbing golden manhood. My hand moves down, almost as if it has a mind of its own, and slides between my legs. I moan as my fingers caress my swollen clit, coating them in the evidence of my growing arousal.

Mothman kneels down between my knees, the forest floor crunching beneath his powerful frame. I hold out my glistening fingers for him. Does he understand my yearning?

Mothman looks down at my outstretched fingers. Slowly, almost hesitantly, he extends his long black tongue. It unfurls like a ribbon, gently curling around my hand. The texture is soft and velvety, enveloping my fingers in its warm, moist embrace. I gasp at the intimate caress, my eyes rolling back in ecstasy.

He begins to lick, his tongue undulating over my fingers, lapping up every drop of my essence. The sensations shoot straight to my core and I shudder. He continues his ministrations, dragging his tongue along each finger before sucking them into his mouth. The suction causes me to cry out, my voice echoing through the silent forest. I'm lost in the hypnotic rhythm of his licks and sucks. My arousal heightens with each pass of his dexterous tongue.

I'm whimpering now, desperate for more contact. Mothman seems to sense this. With one final suck, he releases my fingers from his mouth. A thin strand of saliva connects us for a brief moment before breaking.

I don't know how to explain it, but I can *feel* him asking for permission. He wants me, but he needs me to consent.

I spread my legs as wide as I can, parting my pussy lips with one hand. Please let him understand. Please let me take me.

A shiver courses through my spine as Mothman stares at my exposed sex. Slowly, he inches closer, the air around me warming from his body heat. His intoxicating musk, a heady mix of forest and earth, fills my nostrils.

His long tongue unfurls again, but instead of touching me where I expect, it runs up my inner thigh, teasing and tickling. I gasp, my hips arching upwards, silently begging for more. Slowly, agonizingly, he begins to trace patterns on my thighs, his tongue leaving a trail of fire in its wake.

The anticipation is killing me. I'm so close to the edge already, but I want more. I need more.

"Please," I whimper, my voice barely a whisper. "I need you."

That's all the invitation he needs. Mothman's tongue slides up my thigh and I bite my lip again, trying to maintain some modicum of control, but it's no use. Finally, when his tongue reaches its destination I fall onto my back and let out an almighty scream of pleasure.

He laps at my engorged clit, slowly, sensually, as if he has all the time in the world. I groan, my hips bucking against his skilled tongue. His grip on my thighs tighten, his claws digging in just enough to leave behind a memento of our encounter. The slight sting of pain only heightens my pleasure.

His tongue flicks over my swollen clit again and again, tracing delicate circles around the throbbing nub before dipping inside my wet entrance. His tongue is warm and wet, filling me in a way nothing else ever could. I moan, my hands grabbing fistfuls of the damp forest floor, nails clawing at the soft earth. His tongue plunges deeper, curling and twisting inside me, coating every inch of my quivering passage in his velvety warmth. The sensations are so intense, so foreign, yet so right. I've never felt anything like it, and I know I'll never want anything else again. No man, woman, or anyone else will please me the way Mothman does.

As his tongue delves deeper, I feel a pressure building within me, tightening like a coiled spring ready to burst free.

I'm close, so close to release.

Mothman withdraws his tongue, but before I can protest he dives in again. This time he uses his dexterous tongue to circle my tight rim, teasing me with featherlight flicks. I moan wantonly, all inhibitions gone.

"Please, oh god, please," I moan needily.

His long tongue laps at my puckered hole, tracing delicate patterns that have me writhing beneath him. When the tip finally breaches my ass, I climax instantly. Wave upon wave of pleasure pulls me under so that I can hardly breathe.

My vision whites out as I feel his long snaking tongue dance in my ass, and then slowly retreat. I can feel my slick juices running down my thighs and I'm sure I look a mess, but I don't care. I've never felt more alive or more satisfied in my entire life.

Mothman stands, towering above me, his chest heaving and his amber cock bobbing hypnotically. His glowing red eyes bore into mine, and I swear he's trying to tell me something. Then, with a single beat of his massive wings, he takes to the sky, disappearing into the inky blackness of the night.

I lay there, gasping for air, my body still tingling from our forbidden union.

I look around for Steve, half expecting to see his cowering form watching me from a bush. But he's not there. Only a trail of blood leading off into the forest indicates he was ever there at all.

Chapter Three

So, you're probably wondering what happened to Steve. I'm not proud to admit this, but I left him. Assuming there was anything left of him to leave... There was a lot of blood and not a whole of Steve. Poor guy. He just wanted to get his dick wet, not get eaten by a famous cryptid.

"Sarah... Earth to Sarah... Are you ok?"

A hand wafts in front of my face and I blink a few times, pulling myself back to reality. It's Jessica, a work buddy who's on shift with me today.

"Yeah, sorry... I just zoned out for a minute. I'm ok."

"You've been up all night with Mothman haven't you?" Jessica says with a mischievous smile. "It's exciting isn't it?"

My heart skips a beat, then starts racing like a hummingbird on cocaine. How the fuck does Jessica know about last night? Did she see something? Oh god, is there blood on me? I took a shower before coming in today.

I force a laugh, trying to keep my voice steady. "Mothman? Come on, Jess, you don't really believe in that stuff do you?"

Jessica leans in, her eyes sparkling with excitement. "Ohhh, didn't you hear? There were sightings all over town last night. Red eyes in the dark, strange noises... Some people even claim they saw him flying!"

I swallow hard, my throat suddenly dry. "Really?" My voice comes out higher-pitched than usual. Jessica doesn't seem to notice.

"Oh yeah! It's all over the news. Social media's going wild, too. Everyone's saying it's the real deal." She grins and wiggles her fingers at me, mock-spooky. "You didn't happen to go looking for him last night, did you?"

"Me?" I scoff. "No way. I was home. Watching TV. Super boring stuff. You know me, early to bed, early to rise."

Jessica gives me a once-over, her eyebrow arching skeptically. "Uh-huh. Sure. You're staring into space like someone who definitely got a full eight hours."

I shrug, trying to deflect. "I'm just tired. Long day already, you know?"

Jessica isn't convinced. She narrows her eyes, studying me. "I mean, you're our resident spooky chick, right? And you're telling me you didn't hear *anything* about the sightings?"

I fumble with a pen on the check-in desk, trying to look busy. "Guess I'm slacking on my cryptid news," I mumble. "Sorry."

She plops down in the chair next to me, her excitement undeterred. "Seriously, though. People are saying it's not just a prank this time. I mean, deep scratches on buildings, weird shadows on CCTV — it's got to be Mothman, right?"

"I think people see what they want to see," I reply, shrugging. But inside, I'm sweating bullets. Scratches on buildings?! CCTV footage?!

Jessica laughs. "You're no fun. Lunch later?"

"Sure," I say, managing a weak smile.

As she leaves, my heart finally slows, but my brain is already spinning. Sightings. Scratch marks. I need to get to my phone.

And maybe a therapist.

I reach under the check-in desk and grab my phone from its hiding spot. It's technically against the rules to have it out during work hours, but let's face it – we all do it.

I glance around the lobby. It's quiet, just the faint hum of the air conditioner and the squeak of the janitor's cart down the hall. No customers. Perfect.

My fingers fly across the screen as I open the browser.

Mothman sightings. Last night. McClintic Wildlife Management Area.

It's almost too easy – my search pulls up dozens of results. Local news sites, forums, Reddit threads. Everyone in town seems to have something to say about last night's 'event'.

I scroll past the generic headlines like '*Mysterious Red Eyes Seen in the Dark*' and '*Mothman Returns to Point Pleasant*'. Then I see it – a headline that makes my heart stop.

'*When Cosplay Goes Cryptid: Man Claims Real Mothman Attack!*'

My mouth goes dry as I click the link. The page loads slowly, taunting me, but when it finally pops up, my eyes devour every word.

"Cosplayer and cryptid enthusiast, Steve Myers, was hospitalized early this morning following a bizarre incident near the McClintic Wildlife Management Area. According to Myers, he ventured into the area alone after leaving the Point Pleasant Cosplay Convention, hoping to 'hunt for evidence' of the legendary Mothman. Myers, who was dressed in a Mothman costume at the time, claims he was attacked by a creature he describes as 'larger than life' with glowing red eyes and immense wings. Myers was discovered hours later by a passing motorist, staggering along the side of the road with deep lacerations across his back. He was rushed to the hospital, where he is expected to make a full recovery. Authorities have not yet confirmed the nature of the attack but are investigating the area for signs of wildlife or other potential causes. When asked about the incident, Myers insisted, 'It wasn't an animal. It was him. Mothman. And he was pissed.'"

My grip on the phone tightens. Steve's alive. He's alive!

I scan the article for more details, but most of it is filler – background information on Mothman lore, quotes from so-called eyewitnesses, and speculation about Steve's costume attracting the cryptid. No mention of me, thank god. No mention of... well, anything else that happened last night.

But the lacerations? My stomach churns. Those weren't part of the plan. Poor dude.

I lock my phone and slide it back under the desk. My thoughts are a whirlwind. Relief. Guilt. Panic. And somewhere in the chaos, a tiny spark of something else... Pleasure? Anticipation?

Arousal.

Now that I know Steve is ok I don't have to feel guilty. I can admit to myself that last night was... It was... Well, fuck. It was the best sex of my life. The way his tongue felt against my thigh, my clit, deep in my ass.

I squeeze my thighs together, trying to quell the heat building between them. This is not the time nor place for those kinds of thoughts. I'm at work, for fuck's sake. But the memories flood back unbidden – his smoldering eyes, his contoured abs, his amber cock.

I squeeze my eyes shut, trying to banish the images, but they only grow more vivid.

The way he stared at my exposed, wet cunt.

A soft moan escapes my lips before I can stop it. My cheeks burn as I glance around, praying no one heard. The lobby is still mercifully empty.

I shift in my chair, trying to ignore the growing ache between my legs. But it's no use. The memories of last night flood my senses, as vivid as if they were happening all over again.

My hand slides down, almost of its own accord. I know I shouldn't. Not here. Not now. But I can't help myself.

I glance around once more, making sure the coast is clear. Then, slowly, I let my fingers drift under the desk, and I pull up my skirt.

The smooth wood of the check-in desk conceals my movements as I start to rub slow circles over my clit. My breath quickens, the fabric of my panties already damp. I bite my lip to stifle a gasp as I trace lazy circles over and over.

I'm back in the woods, the cool night air kissing my skin. But this time, there's no fear. Only raw, primal desire. I remember his massive wings unfurling, blocking out the moonlight. The way his glowing red eyes raked over my body, hungry and inhuman.

My fingers move faster as I recall how his long, prehensile tongue explored my folds. I can almost feel the soft, velvety texture of his tongue as it delved deeper, probing places no human could reach.

My hips rock subtly against my hand, chasing that delicious friction. I'm close now, teetering on the edge. My muscles tense, my toes curl in my shoes. Just a little more...

The soft whoosh of the automatic doors snaps me back to reality. A middle-aged couple strolls into the lobby, suitcases in tow. I yank my hand away from my crotch before the first wave of my orgasm hits. The couple approaches the desk, and I plaster on my best customer service smile, praying they can't see the flush in my cheeks or hear the quiver in my voice.

"Welcome to the Point Pleasant Hotel," I manage to say, my voice only slightly breathless. "How can I help you today?"

The couple smiles politely, oblivious to what happened just moments ago. As I go through the motions of checking them in, one thing is clear: I have to see him again. Mothman. My winged lover. My beautiful monster.

Chapter Four

The gravel crunches under my tires as I pull into the empty parking lot. The McClintic Wildlife Management Area feels different tonight – heavier, like the air itself is holding its breath. The shadows are longer, stretching like black ribbons across the cracked concrete. The trees seem to lean closer, their branches clawing at the edges of my vision.

The car radio crackles as the weatherman makes his announcement: "A severe thunderstorm warning is in effect for the area. Expect high winds, heavy rain, and frequent lightning."

I reach out and twist the dial, silencing him.

"Thanks for the pep talk, buddy," I mutter. "Really setting the mood."

I park near the edge of the lot, the treeline looming just ahead like a dark wall of tangled branches and secrets. I sit there for a moment, gripping the steering wheel like it's the only thing keeping me grounded. I could walk back to the clearing where it happened – where I saw him, felt him – but if the weatherman is right, I should probably stick close to the car.

I step out and lean against the hood, the warm metal pressing into my back as I tilt my head to the sky. It's still clear for now, stars flickering faintly above.

"Alright, Mothman," I say under my breath, half-joking, half-desperate. "I'm here. Again. If you're gonna show up, now's the time. Preferably before the storm hits, because I did *not* dress for a biblical flood."

A faint rustling in the trees catches my attention, and my heart kicks into overdrive. I squint into the darkness, trying to make out any movement.

I take a tentative step toward the treeline, drawn by an inexplicable pull – a mix of curiosity, longing, and something I can't quite name. My fingers tremble as I unbutton my blouse, letting it fall open. The night air brushes against my skin, cool and electric.

The rustling grows louder, closer, and my breath catches in my throat. My pulse thrums in my ears. This is it. This has to be it.

But then, a raccoon waddles out of the underbrush, its masked face peering up at me with what I can only describe as judgment.

"Of course," I mutter, followed by a shaky laugh. "Just a raccoon. Because why wouldn't it be?"

The magic of the moment evaporates like mist in sunlight, leaving me feeling exposed and foolish. With trembling fingers, I re-button my blouse. My cheeks burn with embarrassment.

What was I thinking, coming out here like this? Chasing shadows and exposing myself to raccoons...

I turn back to my car, my boots crunching against the gravel. The stars above seem dimmer now, their light swallowed by the weight of my own disappointment. Maybe this was a mistake. Maybe I'm just chasing shadows and impossible dreams.

I hoist myself onto the hood, the metal still warm from the engine. Lying back, I stare up at the star-speckled sky, trying to recapture that earlier spark. But it's no use. It's gone.

I watch the sky intently, scanning for any sign of movement against the tapestry of stars. My eyes dart from constellation to constellation, searching for a dark shape interrupting their ancient patterns. The longer I stare, the more the pinpricks of light seem to swirl and dance, playing tricks on my desperate mind.

With a hopeless sigh, I look away from the sky and pull out my phone. The blue glow illuminates my face as I type "moth" into the search bar. I scroll through countless images – delicate wings in muted browns and greys, feathery antennae, compound eyes.

My fingers fly across the screen as I devour every scrap of information. Did you know some moths can detect sound frequencies up to 300 kHz? Or that the Atlas moth's wingspan can reach nearly a foot across? I learn about pheromones and silk production, about nocturnal navigation, and camouflage techniques.

Wait! *Pheromones?*

The word sparks something in my mind, a fragmented memory from a long-ago biology class. I can almost hear my high school teacher droning on about chemical signals and mating rituals. My heart races as I dive deeper.

Female moths, I learn, release pheromones – powerful scent molecules that can attract males from miles away. These airborne messengers carry coded information about species, readiness to mate, and even the quality of the female's genes. The right smell is like an irresistible siren song that can draw male moths from miles and miles away.

Of course! That's it! Last night, when I was having sex with Steve, I was letting off pheromones! And if a tiny moth can detect such subtle chemical signals, imagine what a human-sized moth can detect!

I hastily unbutton my blouse again, fingers fumbling in my eagerness. The cool night air hits my skin, and I feel my nipples harden beneath the fabric of my bra. A thrill runs through me as I hike up my skirt, exposing my thighs to the moonlight. Time to finish what I started at work earlier!

My hand slides between my legs. I close my eyes and try to relax, losing myself in the sensations. I imagine pheromones billowing from my body in great clouds, filling the night air with an irresistible perfume. In my mind's eye, I see it drifting through the trees. Curling tendrils of scent carried on the breeze.

I picture him out there in the darkness, those enormous wings unfurling as he catches my scent. His antennae twitch, sampling the air.

My fingers work faster, circling and pressing as I imagine him taking flight. In my mind's eye, I see his massive form gliding silently through the forest, drawn inexorably toward me.

My breath comes in ragged gasps as pleasure builds.

I can almost feel those feathery antennae brushing against my skin as my fingers work faster, circling and pressing. My hips buck against my hand as I imagine his colossal form looming over me, drawn by my primal scent.

A low moan escapes my lips, echoing in the empty parking lot.

I imagine him out there, those compound eyes gleaming in the darkness. Does he see in ultraviolet, picking up hidden patterns on my skin? Can he sense the heat radiating from my body, like a beacon in the night?

I'm so wet now, my arousal coating my thighs. The night air feels electric against my fevered skin. Every breeze, every rustle of leaves sends shivers through me. I'm hyper-aware of every sensation – the cool metal beneath me, the whisper of fabric as I shift, the pulsing ache between my legs.

I slide two fingers inside, lost in the fantasy. I imagine his massive form descending from the sky, blocking out the stars as he hovers above me. Those impossibly large wings create gusts of wind that make my hair whip around my face.

My fingers move faster, matching the frantic beating of my heart.

I picture his tongue unfurling, impossibly long. It snakes down my body, leaving a trail of tingling sensation in its wake. When it reaches the junction of my thighs, I cry out, teetering on the edge of release.

My back arches off the car hood as waves of pleasure course through me. I cry out into the night, not caring who might hear. Let the whole forest know what I'm doing, what I'm offering.

A crack of thunder answers my orgasmic pleas, startling me back to reality. My eyes fly open as fat raindrops begin to splatter against my overheated skin. The storm the weatherman promised has arrived with a vengeance.

I scramble off the hood, fumbling with my clothes as the rain intensifies. Lightning flashes, illuminating the parking lot in stark relief. For a moment, I swear I see an enormous winged silhouette against the treeline, but it's gone in an instant.

My heart pounds as I yank open the car door and throw myself inside, slamming it shut behind me. Rain lashes against the windshield as I struggle to catch my breath. Did I really see something out there, or was it just a trick of the light?

There's another flash of lightning, but this time I'm sure – there's nothing there except the forest. It's time to give up and go home.

Chapter Five

Holy crap, I can't see a thing out there. The rain is coming down in sheets so thick my windshield wipers might as well be toothpicks scraping against glass. Every few seconds, a flash of lightning illuminates the road ahead, but that almost makes it worse – the sudden brightness leaves me even more blind than before.

I lean forward, squinting through the windshield like that'll somehow help. My hands are starting to ache from gripping the steering wheel so hard, but I don't dare loosen them. Not with the way my little Honda is being tossed around by the wind. Each gust feels like it might send me spinning off into the darkness.

"Just five more miles," I mutter to myself, trying to remember the curve of this back road. "Five more miles and you're home, Sarah. Just you, your car, and a hurricane. No big deal."

Another blast of wind rocks the car, and I feel my shoulders climb up toward my ears. The radio crackles with static between weather alerts.

"Severe weather in the area."

No kidding, buddy. Thanks for the update.

That's when I see it – a massive, dark shape looming directly in my headlights. My heart stops.

Time slows, then snaps forward.

My foot slams the brake pedal so hard it jolts up my leg. The tires screech, but the road is a river of rain. The car hydroplanes, skidding, spinning. I'm screaming, gripping the wheel like it can save me.

A horrible *thud* shakes the car, the impact shuddering through my bones. The world tilts, metal groans, and then-

Silence.

Just the drum of rain on the roof and my own ragged breathing, too loud in the stillness.

Oh god. Oh god, I hit something. Someone.

I can't move. My hands won't let go of the steering wheel. The windshield wipers keep sweeping back and forth, back and forth, but they're not clearing away the horrible reality of what just happened.

I hit someone. There was a person, and I hit them, and oh god, what if they're dead?

My breath comes in short, shallow gasps, each one clawing its way out of my chest. My mind races, spiraling through headlines I might see tomorrow: 'Local Woman Kills Pedestrian in Storm' and 'Reckless Driver Sentenced to Life'. They'll arrest me. I'll go to prison. My whole life, over, because I was too stubborn to pull over and wait out the storm. Because I thought I could outrun it.

My hands are shaking so badly it takes three tries to unbuckle my seatbelt. The click feels deafening in the silence of the car. When I finally push open the door, the wind slams into it, nearly ripping it from my grip. Rain lashes at me, icy and relentless, soaking through my sweater in seconds. It clings to my skin, heavy and cold.

Lightning splits the sky, illuminating the road in a blinding flash. That's when I see it – a large, dark shape crumpled on the asphalt about twenty feet behind my car. My stomach lurches.

Fuck.

I take a step forward, then another, my legs unsteady. The rain stings my face, and the wind howls in my ears, but all I can focus on is the shape ahead. The shape that shouldn't be there. The shape that might be a person.

My legs feel like jelly but I force myself to keep walking. The beam from my car's tail lights catches something that looks like fur.

Oh, god. It's you.

I drop to my knees beside him, rain pelting my back. Those massive wings from last night are spread across the wet asphalt like broken umbrellas. In the dim red glow of my tail lights, I can see dark liquid mixing with rainwater. Blood? My stomach lurches.

He looks so different unconscious. Without those glowing red eyes, without the otherworldly presence that had both terrified and thrilled me that night, he seems almost... fragile. His chest is moving – thank god, he's breathing – but it's shallow and uneven. Dirt and blood mat his dark fur.

"Hey," I whisper, touching his shoulder. No response. "Please wake up. Please be okay."

What am I supposed to do? I can't call an ambulance – they'd turn him into a lab experiment. But I can't just leave him here to die.

Another flash of lightning illuminates his face, and suddenly I'm back in that moment when his tongue explored my hand. The strange, electric feeling of his touch. The way he'd vanished into the night, leaving me with nothing but questions and dreams and an obsession I couldn't shake.

"Okay," I say, straightening my shoulders. "Okay. This is happening. I'm saving the Mothman."

Because really, what else can I do? The universe just literally threw him in my path. And this time, I'm not letting him disappear.

I grab him under the arms and pull. Nothing happens except my feet sliding on the wet asphalt.

"Come on," I grunt, trying again. "You weigh a ton!"

His wings drag behind him like broken kites, catching on every bump in the road. I adjust my grip and manage to move him about two feet before my arms start shaking. The rain isn't helping – everything's slippery, and my hair is plastered to my face, half-blinding me.

A car could come by any minute. The thought sends a surge of panic-fueled strength through me. I hook my arms under his shoulders again and pull with everything I've got. This time he moves. I half-drag, half-slide him toward my car.

Getting him into the backseat is like trying to fold an oversized origami creature into a shoebox. His wings keep catching on the door frame, and I'm terrified of hurting him worse. I push, pull, and awkwardly maneuver until finally – *finally* – he's sprawled across my back seat. His legs are bent at an odd angle, and one wing is kind of crumpled against the window, but he's in.

I slam the door and lean against it, panting. My entire body feels like jelly, and my car's interior looks like I've hosted a mud wrestling match. But none of that matters. What matters is he's safe, he's with me, and this time I'm not letting him vanish into thin air.

Chapter Six

Getting an unconscious cryptid into your house is exactly as difficult as it sounds. Worse, actually, because nobody talks about the logistics of maneuvering eight feet of Mothman through a standard-sized door. Note to self: install wider doors, just in case this becomes a habit.

My couch has seen better days. There's wet fur everywhere, and I'm pretty sure those claw marks on my hardwood floor aren't coming out anytime soon. But at least he's inside, sprawled across my furniture like the world's most improbable houseguest. His wings drape over both armrests, and his legs stretch well past the end of the couch.

The storm that brought him to me (or rather, the storm during which I hit him with my car, but let's not dwell on that) is finally settling into a gentle patter against the windows. In its wake, the house feels unnaturally quiet, like the space between heartbeats. Every now and then, one of his antennae twitches, and I catch myself holding my breath.

I should probably be terrified. There's a creature of urban legend unconscious in my living room, after all. Instead, I find myself mesmerized by the rise and fall of his chest, the way his fur shimmers even in the dim light. It's like having a piece of the night sky stretched out on my sofa.

I need to check his injuries, which means getting close enough to touch him. My hands shake as I approach, but curiosity wins over caution. His fur is softer than it looks, like velvet made from shadows. Beneath it, I can feel the solid mass of muscle – he's built like an Olympic athlete (if Olympic athletes came with wings and exoskeletons).

Speaking of wings... there's a tear in his right one, about the length of my hand. I expected blood, but instead found something altogether more fascinating: a translucent membrane that seems to catch and hold what little light there is, like mother-of-pearl. The edges of the tear are already drawing together, healing faster than should be possible. Every so often it pulses with a faint bioluminescence that makes my breath catch.

I should be taking notes, documenting this for science or something. Instead, I'm fighting the urge to trace the contours of his chest, to explore the point where fur merges into that strange, beautiful skin. This is ridiculous – he's not even human. But there's something about him that draws me in, like a moth to... well, you know.

God, I hope he doesn't wake up and catch me basically feeling him up in his sleep.

Shit! Too late!

Have you ever seen those videos where someone wakes up from surgery, completely disoriented and convinced they're being abducted by aliens? Yeah, it's kind of like that, except I'm dealing with an actual cryptid who probably thinks he's being abducted by humans. Which, technically, he is.

He launches himself off my couch with surprising grace for someone who just regained consciousness, his wings spreading to their full wingspan.

Oops – and there go my curtains!

His eyes are like emergency flares in the dark, scanning the room wildly until they fix on... my reading lamp.

Oh no.

"Hey, big guy, maybe we could just-" But he's already moving, drawn to the light like the moth that he is. He bumps into it head-first with a soft thunk, then circles it with increasing agitation, knocking over my stack of National Geographics in the process. Each wing beat sends papers flying around the room like confetti.

"Hold on!" I lunge for the lamp switch. "Let me just-"

The room plunges into darkness, save for those glowing red eyes. We stare at each other, both breathing hard. His chittering fills the silence. Somehow it reminds me of a cat's purr.

"It's okay," I say softly, not sure if I'm reassuring him or myself. "You're safe here." The chittering changes pitch, becoming softer, almost melodic. I find myself smiling at him. "I'm glad you're ok."

His head tilts, just slightly, and I swear I see those red eyes dim to a softer glow. Maybe we can understand each other after all.

In the dim light from the window, I notice he's favoring his left side.

"Let me help," I whisper, approaching slowly with my first aid kit. He watches me, head tilted, but doesn't move away. My hands tremble slightly as I clean a nasty scrape along his torso. His chittering vibrates through my fingertips where they meet his skin.

I try to focus on the task, but it's impossible to ignore how the muscles beneath his fur tense and relax under my touch. Every time I apply the antiseptic, his wings flutter slightly, creating little currents of air that brush against my face like phantom caresses.

When my fingers accidentally brush against an uninjured patch of his chest, his breath catches – such a human reaction that it startles us both. Our eyes meet, and for a moment, the space between us feels impossibly small. I should step back, but I can't seem to make myself move. His hand – clawed but gentle – comes up to hover near my cheek, not quite touching, as if he's as uncertain about crossing this line as I am.

I clear my throat and step back, suddenly very aware of what I'm doing.

"Right. You need rest." My voice comes out huskier than intended, and I busy myself with gathering blankets from the hall closet. Anything to distract from the lingering warmth where his hand almost touched my face.

The absurdity of the situation hits me as I'm arranging pillows on and around the sofa. I'm making a bed for Mothman. If someone had told me this morning that I'd be playing nurse to a cryptid, I'd have suggested they lay off the late-night conspiracy forums. Yet here I am, trying to figure out if he needs one pillow or two.

I settle for creating a sort of nest on and around the sofa, with enough space for his wings to spread comfortably. He watches every movement I make with an intensity that should be unnerving but somehow isn't. When I gesture to the makeshift bed, he seems to understand, settling into it with surprising grace. Those massive wings fold around him like a living blanket. I wonder what it would feel like to be wrapped in them.

"Well... goodnight, I guess," I manage, backing toward my bedroom. "Try not to knock over any more lamps?"

At my door, I can't help but look back. His eyes glow softly in the darkness, following my every move. As I close my door, I can't shake the feeling that he understands far more than just my gestures. That perhaps, like me, he's been searching for something he didn't even know he was missing until now.

Chapter Seven

You know that moment when you wake up after a night of drinking and reality feels fuzzy, and you're not sure if you actually did something insane – like, say, invite a cryptid to stay overnight? Yeah. That's me right now, stumbling down my hallway at 6AM, half-hoping I'll find my living room empty and my sanity intact.

But no. He's there.

Mothman is curled up in the nest of blankets I made for him last night, his massive wings folded around his body. His chest rises and falls in a slow, steady rhythm that seems almost too deliberate to be natural. The morning light filters through my curtains, catching on the fine edges of his fur.

I stand there, frozen in the doorway.

"Okay, Sarah," I whisper to myself. "This is fine. Totally fine. You've got this."

I don't got this.

"Hey," I whisper, kneeling beside him. No response. I try again, a little louder this time, even daring to gently touch one of his wings. The texture is strange – soft but powdery, like the wings of a real moth but scaled up to human proportions.

He still doesn't respond though. No movement, no reaction. Great. Either I've somehow managed to put him in a coma, or…

Oh.

Moths are nocturnal, dimwit. Of course he's not going to wake up at the crack of dawn – he's probably just settling into his version of deep sleep. I feel a flicker of relief, quickly followed by a wave of embarrassment. How did I not think of that sooner?

This is good, though. I have to go to work. I've already taken off one too many sick days this year. I was worried about leaving him alone, but if he's going to sleep all day it should be fine. Right?

I spend the next hour getting ready for work and tiptoeing around the house. I check in on him one last time before leaving.

"Don't destroy my house while I'm gone," I whisper, lingering in the doorway. He doesn't stir, his chest rising and falling in that slow, steady rhythm. Then, I grab my bag and head out the door, already dreading what will probably be the most distracted workday of my life.

Chapter Eight

The hotel lobby is a madhouse. Cosplayers are everywhere, dragging oversized suitcases and half-dismantled props, their costumes in various states of post-convention collapse. A guy in a crumpled wizard robe has glitter smeared across his cheek like war paint. A woman dressed as a sci-fi soldier struggles to wrangle a prop gun bigger than my torso. And then there's the furry dragon suit – its wearer has to squeeze sideways through the revolving door, nearly causing a pileup in the process.

I smile and check-out guests as quickly as I can, but my brain is barely keeping up. Half of me is still at home, staring at the nest of blankets in my living room and wondering if Mothman's okay. The other half is busy obsessing over what he'll do if he wakes up while I'm gone. What if he gets thirsty? What if he tears up the couch? What if he *eats* the couch?!

"Next!" My voice comes out chipper, but my hands are moving on autopilot, scanning room keys and processing charges while my thoughts spiral. That's when I notice *them*.

There's a lot of them – eight, maybe more – moving as a unit, their black suits cutting through the colorful chaos of the lobby like a knife. They're sharp and efficient, their polished shoes clicking against the tile in perfect, unnerving rhythm. They don't laugh or chat like the cosplayers around them. They don't even seem to notice the chaos. They just move, their eyes scanning the room with a precision that feels almost mechanical.

They make their way to the desk in a line so straight it could've been drawn with a ruler. The air around them feels heavy, like they've brought their own gravity, and the chatter in the lobby seems to dim as they approach.

"Reservation for Clark," one of them says, a man with a voice as smooth as it is cold. He slides his ID across the counter without a smile, his tone clipped and professional, with just a hint of "don't ask questions".

I glance down at the ID, my stomach doing a slow, uncomfortable flip. The name is generic – John Clark – but the photo is… off. There's something uncanny valley about it.

"Of course," I say, typing the name into the system. My hands feel clumsy, and I suddenly wish my name tag didn't exist. His gaze lingers on it just long enough to make my skin crawl.

"Can I just confirm how many rooms?" I ask, my voice slightly higher than usual.

"Four," he replies, curt and efficient, like every word is rationed.

"All sorted. Welcome to the Point Pleasant Hotel," I say, forcing a smile. "Enjoy your stay." My hands are shaking, just slightly, as I slide the keycards across the counter.

They don't respond, just turn in unison and walk away. As they disappear into the elevator, my chest tightens. What are they doing here? They're not cosplayers, that much is obvious. But they're not a regular group of businessmen either. Something about them feels wrong. Like they know something I don't.

I try to shake off the uncomfortable feeling in the pit of my stomach and focus on the next guest – a fairy queen with a glittery tiara and a smile so bright it almost distracts me from the lingering unease. Almost.

But then I notice someone giving me a strange look from further down the line. At first, I think it's my imagination – people glance at me all the time while I'm working, usually impatient for the line to move faster. But this guy is different. His eyes narrow like he's trying to place me. He's wearing a hoodie and jeans, and his brown hair is all over the place – so he's definitely not one of the business suit people – that much is clear.

"You," he says when he finally steps up to the desk. "I know you."

I freeze. "I'm sorry?"

"You're... Sarah, right?" He tilts his head, studying me. "We met the other night. At the, er, wildlife area."

The pieces snap together so quickly I almost drop my pen. Steve! Of course I didn't recognize him – he'd been wearing that stupid mask the whole time.

I glance nervously around the lobby, my heart picking up speed. The men in black suits are nowhere in sight, but I don't want to risk being overheard.

"Uh, could you give me a second?" I ask my colleague before grabbing Steve's wrist and pulling him toward a quiet corner near the vending machines.

"Whoa, what's the rush?" Steve asks, laughing lightly as I glance nervously over my shoulder.

"What do you remember?" I ask, my voice low and urgent. "From that night?"

He shrugs, a cheeky grin spreading across his face. "A lot of screaming. Mine, mostly. Oh, and the part where the actual Mothman showed up and he *fucked* you. That was new."

"Keep your voice down!" I hiss, darting another look toward the lobby. "Do you want everyone to hear you?" I gesture vaguely toward the front desk. "You didn't notice the group of guys in suits? They're obviously the government. Probably Men in Black. "

Steve's grin only widens. "Oh. My. God. You liked it, didn't you?" He leans in, his tone teasing. "And here I was worrying you'd be traumatized or something. You're one freaky chick!"

"It's none of your fucking business what I like and don't like," I snap, my face heating up.

The elevator dings, and a man in a crisp black suit steps out. He's holding a tablet and speaking into an earpiece, his expression as unreadable as stone. His gaze sweeps the lobby – and lands on us. My stomach twists.

Steve turns back to me, his face paling slightly. "Shit. You're not joking."

"No, I'm not joking," I reply, keeping my voice low. "Is he still watching us?"

Steve glances at the man and then back at me. "Yes," he says grinning. "It's like we're in some kind of spy movie. Very cool."

"Cool? Are you kidding me?" I snap, keeping my voice low. "You're going to get us both in trouble if you don't act normal. Just – stop looking so obvious!"

He raises his hands in mock surrender, but the grin doesn't leave his face. "Fine. I'll be subtle, but you have to admit this is pretty wild."

I roll my eyes, but before I can respond, Steve leans in closer, his tone shifting. "I have to go, but..." He hands me a business card. "...in case you want to talk more about whatever *this* is. You're weird, but I like weird."

Before I can respond, he slings his duffel bag over his shoulder and heads for the lobby door. I glance at the business card in my hand. My first instinct is to crumple it up, but I sigh instead, and shove it into my trouser pocket. It's not like I'm going to call him – I have much bigger things to worry about. Like the cryptid sleeping on my couch and the black-suited strangers prowling the lobby. Steve might think this is an adventure, but for me, it feels more like a ticking time bomb.

Chapter Nine

The drive home feels like it's taking forever, even though I'm probably going ten over the speed limit the entire way. My fingers drum against the steering wheel like I'm auditioning for a rock band, and my thoughts are spinning faster than the tires. What if Mothman's awake? What if someone sees him through the windows and calls Animal Control? What if he's freaking out and tearing my house apart? Or, god forbid, trying to leave? With those suits in town, the last thing I need is an eight-foot moth making a break for it down Main Street.

I pull into my driveway, cut the engine, and practically fly out of the car. I fumble with my house key, the lock suddenly deciding it's the perfect time to stage a rebellion against my shaky hands. Finally, the door clicks open, and I step inside.

The house is quiet. Too quiet. My heart pounds as I kick off my shoes, glancing toward the living room where I left him this morning.

He's not on the couch.

For a split second, my stomach drops. My brain conjures every terrible possibility – he escaped, someone took him, or maybe I imagined the whole thing. But then I hear it. A faint thud. Then another.

I follow the sound into the kitchen, and there he is. Mothman. My relief is instant but short-lived as I watch him bump his head against the patio doors.

And again.

And again.

Poor guy, he really is part moth.

"Mothman, stop!" I hiss, grabbing the curtains and yanking them shut. He chitters in what I can only assume is frustration, his wings twitching behind him as he turns to look at me. "We've really got to work on your indoor skills, buddy."

I gently guide him away from the window and towards a stool at the breakfast bar. He seems to understand, settling into the seat with little resistance.

I take a step back, surveying his wounds from last night. It's impossible not to notice the changes. The scrapes and cuts are almost completely gone. The only wound that remains is the tear on his wing, but even that's looking much better.

"You're healing so fast," I whisper, more to myself than to him, my voice filled with a mix of awe and guilt. "But your wing..." My words trail off as I shake my head. "I'm so sorry. I did this to you."

He tilts his head slightly, watching me with those glowing eyes. There's something calm in his gaze, something that makes me wonder if he knows exactly what I'm thinking. But what can I do? How do you help a creature like him?

Just then, a low, gurgling sound fills the kitchen. It takes me a second to realize it's coming from him. His stomach – or whatever moth-people have in place of a stomach – rumbles loudly.

My guilt hits me like a punch to the gut. "Oh, crap," I mutter, running a hand through my hair. "I didn't even think about food. I just left you here all day. What do you even eat? Leaves? Lightbulbs? Oh god, please don't say lightbulbs."

He doesn't respond – not that I expect him to – but the way his glowing red eyes follow my movements makes it feel like he understands.

"Okay," I murmur, rolling up my sleeves. "Let's get you something to eat before you start eating the clothes right out of my closet."

I take a look at what's available in the refrigerator, mentally listing what's still edible (it's been a while since I went grocery shopping). The bag of bread on the counter is mold-free, and there's a carton of eggs in the fridge. It's not exactly gourmet, but it'll do.

"Let's hope you're not a picky eater," I say, grabbing a pan and setting it on the stove. I crack a couple of eggs into the pan, toss some bread into the toaster, and rummage through the fridge for any fruit still good enough to eat. A fruit salad feels like a safe bet. Who doesn't like fruit?

The smell of cooking eggs wafts through the kitchen, and I can feel him behind me. Not just in the obvious way, he's not actually standing behind me. But in a different way, like he's *watching* me.

I glance over my shoulder, and sure enough, he's watching me from his seat at the breakfast bar. His glowing red eyes are locked onto my every move, unblinking and impossibly bright. It's unnerving and oddly thrilling at the same time. Like standing in a spotlight.

"You're going to make me nervous if you keep staring like that," I say lightly, trying to break the tension. Of course, he doesn't answer – just tilts his head slightly, like he's trying to figure me out. I turn back to the stove, my hands suddenly clumsier than usual.

The silence stretches between us, broken only by the faint sound of rain dripping from the gutters outside. He's still sitting in his place, his glowing eyes boring into my skin.

I take a deep breath, steadying myself. My palms are damp, and my heart races like I'm about to confess something scandalous – which, in a way, I guess I am.

"I don't know if you can understand me," I start, my voice soft, trembling at the edges. "But I need to say this anyway." His head tilts slightly, the movement small but deliberate, as if encouraging me to go on. I swallow hard, my words catching in my throat. "That night, when you made love to me... I can't stop thinking about it. About you. About how you made me feel. It's insane, I know it is, but it felt... I don't know. Right? Like it wasn't just some random moment. Like it wasn't just animal instinct. It was like it mattered. Like it was fate."

I pause, my chest tightening as the weight of my own words hits me. The kitchen feels too small suddenly. I turn back to the stove, if only to give myself something to do. The toast pops up, startling me, and I fumble to assemble everything on a plate. It's nothing fancy, but I arrange it carefully, as if the presentation might somehow make up for the chaos in my head.

When I set the plate down on the table, I step back, wiping my hands on a dish towel. My voice is quieter now, almost a whisper. "There you go. Breakfast. Or lunch. Or whatever meal this is for you."

His eyes flicker between me and the plate. He's hesitant, careful, like he's not sure if this is some kind of trap.

"I don't know what we're doing here," I say, my voice cracking unexpectedly. "But I'm glad we're doing it. Even if it is completely ridiculous."

His wings shift, a faint rustling sound, and I swear there's a sense of ease in the way he tilts his head. It's enough to make me believe – just for a moment – that we might actually be figuring this out.

Chapter Ten

The air between us feels charged, like the moment before a storm breaks. I can't explain it, this pull I feel toward him. It's not just physical, though god knows that's part of it. It's something deeper. Something primal. Like my body recognizes his in a way my mind can't quite grasp.

He's not touched his food, choosing to leave the counter and come stand near me. He's close now, so close I can feel the heat radiating from him.

His glowing eyes lock onto mine, and for a moment, I forget how to breathe. There's no hesitation in him, no uncertainty. He moves with a kind of deliberate grace, like he knows exactly what he's doing – and exactly what I want, even if I'm not sure myself.

Should I be scared? Running away? No. I'm exactly where I want to be. I'm standing still, my heart pounding in my chest, my skin tingling with anticipation.

"Do you want this?" I whisper, my voice barely audible. "Do you want me?" It's a stupid question, really. He probably doesn't even understand the words. But I need to say them, if only for myself.

He doesn't answer, of course. Instead, he tilts his head as if he's trying to decipher my meaning. And then, slowly, deliberately, he takes another step closer.

My breath hitches, but I don't back away. Instead, I reach for the hem of my shirt, my fingers trembling as I pull it over my head. The cool air brushes against my skin, raising goosebumps, but I don't stop. I can feel his gaze on me, intense and unblinking, and it sends a shiver down my spine.

I don't know why I'm doing this. Maybe it's the way he's looking at me like I'm the only thing in the world that matters. Maybe it's the memory of that first night, the way he made me feel, the way he still makes me feel. Or maybe it's just the sheer, reckless need to be close to him, to feel that connection again. No matter how strange or dangerous it might be.

My hands move to the clasp of my bra, fumbling for a moment before it comes undone. The straps slide down my shoulders, and I let it fall to the floor. My breath catches again as the cool air kisses my bare skin. I can feel his eyes on me, that unrelenting gaze that seems to see straight through me. Into me. My nipples tighten beneath his scrutiny, hardening into sensitive peaks that ache with need.

I feel a familiar wetness between my thighs and I know, no matter what I say or do, my body is ready for him.

He tilts his head again, those glowing eyes burning into me, and then he moves. Not toward me, but sideways. Circling me like a predator stalking its prey. I turn my head to follow him, but he's always just out of sight, always behind me.

And then he stops. I feel his breath on the back of my neck, warm and uneven. His hands, large and clawed, brush against my sides. His touch is surprisingly gentle, almost reverent, as if he's afraid he might break me.

My fingers tremble as they find the button of my trousers. I pause for a moment, my heart pounding so loud I'm certain he can hear it. My hands slide to the zipper, and I pull it down slowly. The fabric loosens around my hips, and I push the trousers down, letting them pool at my feet. The cool air brushes against my thighs, but it's nothing compared to the heat radiating from him.

His breath hitches, a low, guttural sound that vibrates through the room, through me. I feel it in my chest, in my bones, in the wet, aching core of me. He's so close now, his body a dark shadow looming behind me, and I can feel the heat of him against my bare skin. His claws graze my hips, tracing the curve of my waist, and I bite down on my lip to stifle a moan.

And then he does something I don't expect. He leans forward, his nose brushing against the nape of my neck. He inhales deeply, a long, deliberate sniff that sends a jolt of electricity straight to my core.

He can smell me.

The realization hits me like a lightning strike, and I feel a flush of heat spread across my face and down my chest. He can smell my arousal. The slick, undeniable evidence of how much I want him. How much my body craves him.

His claws tighten on my hips, the sharp points dimpling my skin. A low growl rumbles from his chest, vibrating against my back. The sound is primal, possessive – it speaks to something deep and ancient within me. My body responds instinctively, arching back against him. My head falls back, exposing the vulnerable line of my throat.

His tongue, soft and hot, drags along my neck. I whimper, my fingers clawing at nothing. He tastes me, savoring, learning. When his fangs graze my pulse point, I cry out, a desperate, needy sound.

"Please," I whisper.

His fangs press harder against my throat, not quite breaking the skin, but promising more. I gasp, my body trembling with a mixture of fear and desperate arousal. His claws slide lower, hooking into the waistband of my panties. With a swift motion, he tears them away, leaving me completely bare and exposed.

I should be terrified. This creature, this being of myth and shadow, could tear me apart in an instant. But all I feel is an overwhelming need. A hunger that threatens to consume me from the inside out.

One clawed hand slides between my thighs. His touch is electric, sending shockwaves of pleasure through my body. I gasp and push against him as his claws delicately part my folds, exploring my most intimate places with exquisite care.

I'm trembling now, caught between fear and desperate need. His fangs are still at my throat – a constant reminder of the danger, of how easily he could hurt me. But instead, he's touching me with such reverence, such careful desire.

His fingers find my clit, circling it with agonizing slowness. I cry out, my hips bucking involuntarily against his hand. His other arm wraps around my waist, holding me steady as he explores.

I'm lost in sensation. Drowning in pleasure and fear and need. His claws are dangerously sharp against my sensitive flesh, but he wields them with impossible precision. Each stroke sends jolts of electricity through my body, building a pressure low in my belly that threatens to overwhelm me.

Slowly, he releases his fangs from my neck. Then his tongue, like velvet dipped in fire, slides down my spine. I shudder violently, my breath hitching as his claws continue their relentless exploration between my thighs. The sharpness of them is a constant reminder of his power, his control.

He pauses for a moment at the small of my back. The sensation is unbearable and exquisite all at once – a paradox of pleasure that makes my skin prickle and my mind unravel. Then he moves lower, tracing the curve of my ass. I gasp, my fingers curling into fists as he spreads me open, exposing me completely.

The first touch of his wicked, serpentine tongue is electric. I cry out, pushing my pussy against him as he delves deeper, tasting me with a hunger that borders on obscene.

My body is a live wire, every nerve ending alight with the intensity of his touch. His tongue snakes deeper, curling inside me with a relentless rhythm that has me moaning, pleading for more. The sound is raw, primal, and it only seems to spur him on. His growl reverberates through me, low and possessive, as he drinks me in like I'm the only sustenance he's ever craved.

His tongue retreats. I whimper at the loss, my hips instinctively chasing after him. But he doesn't stop – not really. His tongue trails upward, slick and sinuous, tracing a path along my sensitive skin. It glides over the curve of my ass, teasing the delicate flesh there before sliding up the dip of my spine. I shiver uncontrollably as his tongue moves higher, tracing each vertebra with painstaking precision. One of his arms remains wrapped around me, holding me steady. I'm trembling so violently, I'm not sure I could stand without him.

His tongue, which had been exploring the curve of my shoulder, trails upward. When it reaches the sensitive spot just below my ear, he pauses. Then, with a feather-light touch, his tongue flicks against the shell of my ear. I gasp, my knees buckling slightly. The sensation is intimate, almost teasing.

And then he pushes further.

I gasp, my hands instinctively try to grab at him, but his arms are wrapped so tightly around me that I can't move. His tongue slips deeper into my ear. I feel him reaching further, deeper. Past my skin, past my bone.

It's not just his tongue anymore – it's something more, something that defies explanation. A tendril of warmth, of pressure, of presence, winding its way into me, curling around the edges of my mind. My breath hitches, my body trembling as the sensation floods me, a mix of pleasure and something darker. Something that feels like it's unraveling me from the inside out.

My body arches against his, a low moan escaping my lips as the intensity builds. Wave after wave of something I can't name. It's too much, too strange, too everything, and yet I can't pull away.

His clawed hand continues its frantic circling of my clit as his tongue delves deeper into my mind, weaving itself into the fabric of my consciousness. I can feel him there, not just physically, but in the very core of who I am. His presence is vast, ancient, and utterly consuming. It's as if he's unraveling me, peeling back layers of myself I didn't even know existed, exposing the raw, trembling core beneath.

His claws never cease their maddening rhythm against my clit, each stroke sending jolts of pleasure that seem to echo through my entire being. I'm caught in a paradox – of pleasure and pain, of ecstasy and terror – and I can't tell where one ends and the other begins. My breath comes in ragged gasps, my body writhing in his grasp, but he holds me firm. Unyielding.

"Wait," I manage to choke out, though my voice doesn't sound like my own. It's shaky, breathless, and I'm not even sure what I'm asking him to wait for. To stop? To keep going? I don't know. All I know is that I'm teetering on the edge of something,

something vast and unknowable, and I'm not sure I'm ready for it.

But he doesn't stop. His hands tighten on my shoulders, steadying me as his tongue presses deeper. I feel myself giving in, surrendering to the strange, overwhelming pleasure of it. My mind is a blur, my body trembling, and somewhere in the chaos, I realize I don't want him to stop. I want to see where this goes, even if it scares me. Even if it changes me.

My body convulses violently, an orgasm crashing over me like a tsunami. It's unlike anything I've ever experienced – raw, primal, and all-encompassing. I scream, but I make no sound.

Darkness rushes up to meet me, thick and velvety, wrapping around my limbs like a shroud. I feel myself falling into a black, endless void.

Am I dead?

Do I care?

And then, I hear it.

A voice.

A voice I recognise although I've never heard it.

It's him.

It's Mothman.

Chapter Eleven

I wake up to the soft hum of the night, the glow of the TV on my face. It appears I'm on the couch in my living room... How did I get on the couch? The last thing I remember was standing in the kitchen and then-

Oh god.

The memories come rushing back in jagged pieces. Coming home. Making dinner for Mothman. And trying to seduce him.

Did it work? I can't remember...

Wait.

Yes, it did.

It *definitely* worked.

The details start to flood back, and I feel my face heat up as I replay the moment. His glowing eyes locked onto mine, that strange, magnetic pull between us. The way his breath felt against my skin. And that tongue!

For a moment, I let myself linger on the memory, the heat of it, the way it felt like we were the only two beings in the universe. It was hot. Like, really hot. And not just because he's built like a winged Adonis. There was something about the way he touched me, the way he looked at me, that made me feel seen in a way I didn't know I needed.

But then I remember the ear thing.

My hand flies to the side of my head, half expecting to feel some kind of dried blood or, I don't know, seeping brains. But there's nothing. Just my regular old ear, intact and unremarkable. I feel totally normal. Better than normal, actually, which is weird considering I just had my skull douched out. It's a feeling I can't quite put into words. It's like I've been reset somehow. Weirdly great, but also, bit of an extreme way to go about it.

I imagine most people would tell me to leave the house, get a gun, and maybe call an exorcist. But honestly? I don't think he was trying to kill me. If Mothman wanted me dead, I'd be dead already. It's not like I put up much of a fight, I was gagging for it. Whatever that ear thing was, it wasn't violence. But I don't think it was sex either...

I run my fingers through my hair as the last fragment of the night rushes back: the voice. Deep, resonant, and unmistakably his. But that can't be right. Mothman doesn't talk. Mothman *can't* talk. Right?

I squeeze my eyes shut, trying to replay the memory, but it's slippery, like trying to hold onto a fish. Did I imagine it? Was it some weird, post-brain-douching hallucination?

My mind races, flipping through every possibility, but none of them make sense. Cryptids don't just start chatting in English over breakfast. Then again, cryptids aren't supposed to stick their tongues in your brain either, so maybe I need to adjust my expectations.

There's a noise, and I turn to see Mothman standing sheepishly by the door. When he notices me looking, he steps inside, his movements deliberate but hesitant, like he's not sure if he's welcome. He walks around to the couch, his wings folded tightly against his back.

"Sarah," he says, his voice deep and resonant, each word carefully measured. "You are awake."

I blink, my brain scrambling to catch up. His voice is oddly clear, but there's a strange, halting rhythm to his speech, like he's choosing each word with the precision of someone reading from a dictionary.

Before I can respond, he kneels in front of the couch, his glowing eyes fixed on mine. He takes my hands in his.

"I feel I must apologize," he says, his tone formal but sincere. "What I did earlier was invasive, but necessary. I acted without your consent, and for that, I am deeply sorry. I hope I did not frighten you."

I stare at him, my mouth hanging open.

"So I *did* hear your voice! How is this possible?"

"If you will permit me a moment to explain," he says, his wings twitching slightly behind him. "Through rigorous study, I have learned to understand American English, as well as several other outer-earth languages. I appreciate, however, that my manner of speaking is foreign to your kind. To bridge this gap,

I had to rewire your brain, so that we might understand one another."

I stare at him, unblinking. *Rewire my brain?!* Christ on a cracker. Did he just casually drop that in like it's no big deal?

But then it hits me. I'm not speaking English right now. I'm not even *hearing* English. The words coming out of my mouth – and his – are a series of chitters, clicks, and chirps. Moth-speak. And somehow, I understand it.

"Wait, wait, wait," I say, pulling my hands from his. "Are you telling me I'm speaking *moth* right now?"

He nods, his expression earnest.

"Yes. But do not panic. You may speak in English whenever you wish. I understand both."

I open my mouth, then close it again, my brain short-circuiting.

He tilts his head as if he's trying to understand my reaction. "I did all that I could to make it pleasurable for you."

"Pleasurable?!" I blurt out, my face heating up.

His wings give a slight flutter, and there's a hint of amusement in his voice. "Your moans and physical feedback gave me the distinct impression you were having a good time."

I feel my face go from warm to nuclear. "Oh my god," I mutter, burying my face in my hands. "This is not happening."

He continues, his tone softening. "In the moment, I felt I had no other choice. After what you said... when you were cooking dinner... about how you felt about me..." His voice falters, and he looks down, suddenly hesitant. "I felt compelled to communicate. So I could tell you that I..." He pauses, his glowing eyes flicking up to meet mine.

I can feel my heartbeat in my throat, my breath catching. "That you what?" I whisper, leaning closer, unable to stop myself.

He hesitates, his wings giving a nervous flutter. "That I... am allergic to eggs."

I blink. Once. Twice. "What?"

"The meal you prepared," he says, his voice earnest. "It contained eggs."

I stare at him, my brain struggling to process this.

"Wait. You're telling me you stuck your tongue in my brain, rewired my entire nervous system, and risked giving me a stroke, to tell me you're allergic to eggs?"

He shifts uncomfortably, his wings twitching. "It seemed important to clarify."

I bury my face in my hands, torn between laughing and screaming. "Oh my god. This is my life now. This is actually my life."

And then I hear it – a sound I've never heard from him before. It's low and rumbling, almost like a purr, but with a strange, melodic quality. I peek through my fingers to see Mothman's shoulders shaking slightly, his glowing eyes crinkling at the edges. Is he... laughing?

The absurdity of it all hits me like a tidal wave, and before I know it, I'm laughing too. Not just a polite chuckle, but full-on, tears-in-my-eyes, can't-breathe laughter. It's the kind of laugh that comes from sheer disbelief, from the realization that my life has officially become the weirdest rom-com ever written.

When the laughter finally subsides, we're left in a comfortable silence, just looking at each other. It's... nice. Surprisingly nice. And then it hits me – I don't even know his name.

"So," I say, wiping a tear from my eye. "Do you have a name? Or do I just call you Mothman?"

He hesitates, his wings giving a slight flutter. "I do have a name," he says, his voice soft. "But it is... difficult to pronounce in your language. You may call me Thrax, if you wish."

"Thrax," I repeat, testing the name on my tongue. It feels fitting, somehow – strong, a little mysterious, and just the right amount of weird. "Okay, Thrax. Nice to officially meet you." He dips his head in what I can only assume is a respectful nod. "Let's sit and talk," I say, gesturing toward a chair. "I have *a lot* of questions."

Thrax perches carefully on the armchair opposite, his glowing eyes fixed on me. He looks like he's trying not to break the furniture, which is both endearing and a little ridiculous.

"Where do you come from?" I ask, my voice quiet but eager.

"Not... here," he says, struggling to find the right words. "Beneath. Deep beneath."

"Beneath?" I lean forward, intrigued. "Like... underground?"

"Your world," he continues, his claws tapping gently on the edge of the chair as he searches for the right words, "is the outer-world. There is another world, inside this one. My kind lives there. We have done, for a very long time."

Another world inside ours? I've heard people talk about it, but I always thought it was conspiracy theory nonsense.

"So," I say, my elbows resting on my knees. "How exactly did you end up here? On the surface, I mean."

"Your human machines, they were digging. Breaking the earth. In the place you call the TNT area."

I blink, surprised. "The TNT area? That's what people used to call the McClintic Wildlife Management Area. They used to store explosives there in wartime, hence the nickname."

He nods. "Beneath the ground was a tunnel to the inner-earth. At one time it was open, and I flew out."

I frown, trying to piece it together. "So, you're saying the machines accidentally opened the door to your world?"

"Not a door," he corrects. "More like a crack. It was quite small. But it was enough. I was curious. I wanted to see your world. So I... came through."

"Curious, huh?" I raise an eyebrow, a smirk tugging at my lips. "So you're telling me you're basically the cryptid equivalent of a nosy neighbor?"

His wings twitch, and I swear I see a flicker of amusement in his glowing eyes. "I did not intend to stay," he says, his tone softening. "But the crack, it was closed. Sealed when the TNT area became a wildlife preserve. I could not return."

I lean back, processing this. "So you've been stuck here ever since?"

He nods, his gaze dropping. "The outer-earth is... loud. Bright. Unfamiliar. I have tried to adapt. But it is not my home."

I feel a pang of sympathy for him, mixed with a strange sense of awe.

"And the TNT area... that's where people first started seeing you, right? Back in the '60s?"

"Yes," he says, his voice quiet. "I did not mean to be seen. But your kind are very observant."

I snort. "Observant? That's one way to put it. Most people would say 'paranoid.'"

He tilts his head, considering this. "Perhaps. But your stories, your legends – they have made it harder for me to remain hidden."

I chew on my lip, thinking. "So, what? You're just... stuck here? Forever?"

His glowing eyes meet mine, and for a moment, I see something raw and vulnerable in them. "Unless I find another way."

I feel the weight of his words settle over me. "You can stay here," I say, surprising myself with the certainty in my voice. "If you want to, that is. At least until your wing is healed and you can fly again."

The room feels heavy with the weight of his story, and there's a sadness in his eyes that's hard to ignore. I open my mouth to say something – maybe to reassure him again – but a faint sound outside catches my attention.

Tires on wet asphalt.

My gaze flicks to the window, and I see headlights cut through the darkness. A car rolls slowly past the house. I frown. It's late, and my street isn't exactly a hotspot for traffic. Plus, this car is moving really fucking slow... It's probably nothing, just a takeout delivery driver looking for the right house.

Thrax tilts his head, noticing my shift in focus. "What is it?"

"Just a car," I say, trying to sound casual. "Probably someone lost or something."

But then it happens again. The same car, dark and unmarked, passes in the opposite direction. It's like it drove up the street a few houses, turned around, and came right back.

"Thrax," I say quietly, my voice tense. "It's the same car."

His posture changes immediately. His wings twitch, and his body becomes impossibly still, like a predator sensing danger.

"They are... looking," he says, his voice low and edged with something I can't quite place.

"For you?" I ask, my throat dry.

He doesn't answer, but the way his claws grip the edge of the chair tells me everything I need to know.

Minutes pass in uneasy silence, both of us watching the window. Sure enough, a few minutes later, the car comes by a third time. My stomach churns. Who are they? What do they want? And, most importantly – how much do they know?

Chapter Twelve

I can't sit still. My hands are shaking as I double-check the locks, even though I already know they're bolted. I pull the curtains shut, then peek through them anyway, scanning the street outside. The car is gone.

That should be a good thing, right? If they were watching the house, they'd still be there. But my gut tells me otherwise. The feeling of being hunted lingers, crawling over my skin like static electricity.

I start pacing. Back and forth across the living room, my heartbeat loud in my ears.

"They know," I mutter to myself. "They know something. Maybe not that you're here, but they know something."

I hear the soft rustling of wings behind me. Mothman has been silent this whole time, but now, he moves. When I turn to face him, he's standing in the center of the room, watching me with those glowing red eyes.

"You are afraid," he murmurs.

I huff out a laugh that's way too close to hysteria. "Gee, what gave it away?"

He steps closer, slow and deliberate. "We are safe," he says, like it's an absolute fact. "No one will harm you while I am here."

I want to believe that. God, I do. But my mind keeps spinning worst-case scenarios.

"You don't know that," I whisper. "They're out there, watching, waiting–"

Mothman closes the space between us in one smooth motion. His wings arch slightly behind him, framing his massive form.

"I will not let them take you." His voice is soft, steady.

"But it's not me they're coming for." The words come out barely above a whisper, and I wrap my arms around myself, unable to meet those glowing eyes.

There's a long pause. The soft rustle of his wings fills the silence, and when I finally look up, I catch something in his expression – a flicker of something ancient and weary.

"I know," Thrax says quietly. "It's me." His hand – not quite human, not quite monster – hovers near my shoulder before dropping back to his side.

I thought I was keeping him safe by hiding him here. But the truth? The truth is I'm just another chapter in a story that's been going on far longer than I've been alive. I'm just a single heartbeat in an endless hunt. How many others have tried to shelter him across the centuries? How many homes, how many hideaways, how many humans thinking they could outsmart humanity's relentless need to capture what they don't under-stand? Man has been hunting the unexplainable since we first huddled around fires in caves, pointing at shadows in the dark. And here I am, thinking my little suburban home and drawn curtains could somehow end that primal chase.

My heart aches with a sudden, fierce protectiveness. All those years, all those centuries of running, of being hunted. Has anyone ever truly shown him he deserves more?

Without thinking, I reach for his hand. His skin is warm against mine, and those red eyes flare brighter at the contact. I thread my fingers through his, feeling the subtle differences in his anatomy, the way his joints don't quite align with human ones.

"Come with me," I whisper, tugging gently.

He follows, silent and graceful, as I lead him down the darkened hallway to my bedroom. His wings brush the walls, creating soft whispers in the darkness. When I look back, his gaze is fixed on our joined hands.

I pause at my bedroom door, my heart thundering against my ribs. Not from fear, but from something else entirely. Something that feels like falling and flying all at once.

I open the door, leading Thrax into the dimly lit sanctuary of my bedroom. I turn to face him, my breath catching as those luminous eyes meet mine. Without breaking our gaze, I slowly begin to undress.

My fingers tremble as I unbutton my shirt, letting it fall to the floor with a whisper. Thrax's wings twitch, creating soft currents in the still air. I slide my jeans down, stepping out of them, hyper-aware of his intense focus.

I unhook my bra, letting it join the growing pile of discarded clothing. Thrax's eyes widen, glowing brighter as I stand before him in nothing but my panties.

The air between us crackles with something electric, primal. I can feel his gaze like a physical touch, burning into my skin. My breath catches in my throat as I watch his eyes travel down the length of my body, flickering over every curve and imperfection.

Hesitantly, I reach for the hem of my panties, sliding them down my legs. The cool air caresses my damp center, and I blush under his rapt attention. The sight of him, towering over me in the dim light, is enough to make my knees quake. He's so powerful, so otherworldly, and yet here he is... with me.

My eyes are drawn downward, and I gasp softly. His arousal is evident, straining against the strange, velvety texture of his lower body.

I step closer, drawn by an irresistible magnetism. His cock pulses, growing impossibly harder.

My fingers reach out, trembling. My mouth waters. I want to taste him. I want to take that twisted amber cock deep in my throat.

As my fingertips brush his shaft, Thrax gasps, his eyes slamming shut. His wings flutter behind him, as if to steady himself from my touch. The smooth, heated length of him leaping against my palm, hard and demanding. He tilts his head back with a low groan that sends shivers down my spine. Encouraged by his reaction, I wrap my hand around the girth of him and squeeze.

He's harder than any man I've ever known. And larger too. I can barely tear my eyes away from the way his cock throbs in my grip. I'm desperate to know how it would feel between my lips, inside me. My pussy clenches in response to the thought, hot and needy. I want to feel him — all of him – inside every part of me.

I'm about to kneel when Thrax takes a sudden step back. His wings fold tightly against his body, and he averts his gaze. The luminous red of his eyes dims, flickering like dying embers.

"I... I cannot," he whispers, his voice rough with what sounds like shame. I freeze, my hand still outstretched, feeling suddenly small and exposed. Thrax's shoulders hunch, his massive form seeming to shrink before my eyes. "I cannot," Thrax repeats, his voice a low rumble. "We cannot. It is dangerous."

I take a step closer, reaching out to touch his arm. He flinches away, and the pain of rejection lances through me.

"What do you mean, dangerous?" I ask, trying to keep my voice steady.

"My body is not like yours," he begins, each word carefully chosen. "What flows through my veins, what... comes from me... it is not safe for humans."

I furrow my brow, trying to understand. "You mean, like, your blood?"

He shakes his head, still not meeting my eyes. "My seed. It is corrosive to humans. Acidic."

"Your... your semen?" I repeat, trying to process the information. A memory returns, of his precum hissing on the forest floor that first night. I can't help but feel a twinge of relief. It's not me, it's his... anatomy. I want to laugh at the absurdity of it all, but now is not the time. "I see," I manage to say.

Thrax remains where he stands, his back still to me. "I am sorry," he says stiffly. "I did not mean to arouse you and then... disappoint."

"No, Thrax," I say softly, moving closer to him again. "You haven't disappointed me. I understand."

I gently place my hand on his back, between his wings. He tenses for a moment, then slowly relaxes into my touch.

"Turn around," I whisper. "Please look at me." He hesitates, then slowly turns to face me. His glowing eyes meet mine, filled with a mixture of desire and shame. I cup his face in my hands. "You've given me so much pleasure," I murmur. "I want to do the same for you. I can't expect you to tongue my pussy and ass every time and not receive something in return. Is there no other way?" My hands trail down his chest, feeling the strange ridges and planes of his body. He shudders under my touch, his wings quivering. "Tell me what feels good," I breathe. "There must be ways I can pleasure you that are safe."

Thrax's wings twitch, betraying his excitement despite his hesitation. "I... I am not certain," he admits. "No human has ever wanted to touch me this way."

An idea strikes me then. I bite my lip, gathering my courage before speaking. "What about... what about your... you know — back passage? Is there anything acidic that comes out of there?"

Thrax's eyes widen in shock. For a moment, I worry I've offended him. But then I notice the way his wings are trembling, how his breathing has quickened. There's an unmistakable hunger in his gaze.

"No," Thrax says, his voice hoarse. "There is nothing harmful there."

My heart races as I process his words. I lick my lips, suddenly parched. "Then... may I?" I ask, my hands sliding lower down his torso.

Thrax nods, a barely perceptible movement. His wings flare wide, quivering with anticipation. I gently turn him around, drinking in the sight of his broad back, the way his wings connect to his shoulder blades. My fingers trace the junction where flesh meets fur, and he lets out a soft gasp.

Slowly, reverently, I caress down his spine. His skin is warm, alive with an otherworldly energy that makes my fingertips tingle. When I reach the curve of his ass, I pause, giving him a chance to object. Instead, he spreads his legs slightly, inviting me to continue my exploration.

I let my hands wander over the curve of his ass. It's firm and taut beneath my palms. I knead the flesh gently, drawing a low moan from Thrax. Emboldened, I massage more firmly, working my fingers into the muscle. His wings flutter, sending soft currents of air across my skin.

"Does this feel good?" I murmur.

"Yes," Thrax breathes, his voice thick with pleasure.

"Kneel on the bed," I whisper, my voice husky with desire. "On your hands and knees." Thrax obeys, his movements graceful despite his size. He settles onto the bed, wings folded against his back. The sight of him like this - vulnerable, trusting - makes my heart race. I climb onto the bed behind him, running my hands along his thighs. "Tell me if you want me to stop," I say softly.

I part his cheeks gently, revealing his puckered entrance. It's darker than human flesh, with an iridescent sheen. I lean in, breathing in his musky scent. My tongue darts out, tasting him tentatively.

Thrax gasps, his whole body shuddering. Encouraged, I lap at him more firmly, circling his rim with the tip of my tongue. His wings twitch and flutter as I work, soft chirping sounds escaping him.

I continue lapping at Thrax's entrance, my tongue swirling and probing. I alternate between broad, flat strokes and pointed jabs, feeling him relax further with each pass.

"Please," Thrax groans, pushing back against my face. "More."

I pull back slightly, admiring how his entrance glistens with my saliva. Gently, I press the pad of my index finger against his opening. He tenses for a moment, then consciously relaxes.

I work my finger in slowly, marveling at the tight heat enveloping it. Thrax lets out a low, keening sound as I push deeper. His wings shudder and spread wide, nearly brushing the walls of my bedroom.

"Is this okay?" I whisper, stilling my movements.

"Yes," he gasps. "Please, do not stop."

Encouraged, I begin to curl my finger. His inner walls clench and pulse around me. I probe, gently, searching for that spot that will drive him wild. When I find it, Thrax cries out, his whole body trembling.

"More," he pleads, rocking back against my hand.

I add a second finger, working it in alongside the first. The stretch is tight, but Thrax's body yields to me eagerly. My other hand roams his back, tracing the ridges of his spine and the flesh of his buttocks.

As I continue to massage his delicate ass, I notice Thrax's hand moving beneath him. He's gripping his cock, stroking it in time with the thrusts of my fingers.

I watch, mesmerized, as Thrax pleasures himself. His strange, amber cock glistens in the dim light, pulsing with each stroke of his hand. The sight sends a jolt of arousal through me, my own neglected pussy clenching with need.

"That's it," I murmur, my voice husky. "Stroke that beautiful cock for me." Thrax groans, his wings quivering. I curl my fingers inside him, brushing against that spot that makes him shudder. "Does it feel good?" I ask, my free hand caressing the curve of his ass. "Tell me how it feels."

"Exquisite," Thrax gasps. "I have never... ah!"

I increase the pace. His internal muscles flutter around me, hot and tight.

"That's it," I breathe, my voice husky with desire. "Touch yourself for me. Let me see how good it feels."

Thrax's movements grow more frantic, his hand pumping his cock with increasing urgency. I match his pace, pushing my fingers deeper into his tight heat.

"You're so beautiful like this," I murmur, drinking in the sight of him. "So powerful, so wild. And yet you're letting me inside you, trusting me to make you feel good."

"I am close," he gasps, his voice strained. "I... I cannot..."

"It's okay," I soothe, curling my fingers. "Let go. I've got you."

With a cry that's half-chirp, half-roar, Thrax comes undone. His body convulses, clenching rhythmically around my fingers. I watch in awe as his cock pulses, spraying thick ropes of glowing fluid onto the sheets below. The air fills with a strange, electric scent.

I continue to work my fingers inside him, gently easing him through the aftershocks of his climax. His breathing comes in ragged gasps, his entire body quivering with each exhale.

As the last pulses of his orgasm subside, I become aware of a soft hissing sound. Looking down, I see tendrils of steam rising from the sheets where his seed has landed. The fabric sizzles and bubbles, eaten away by the corrosive cum.

I should probably deal with that before it melts the whole way through... Not now. Not yet. I can't bring myself to care about the damage, not when Thrax is sprawled before me. Utterly spent.

Chapter Thirteen

I'm staring at my alarm clock like it's personally offended me. 6:00AM and I haven't slept more than a couple of hours. My body aches in that peculiar way that comes from staying up way too late doing... well. My cheeks flush at the memory of last night. Let's just say that Mothman and I got better acquainted.

Thrax is sprawled across my bed in a way that shouldn't be possible for someone with wings. One of them drapes over the edge like a gothic curtain, the other curved protectively around his torso. The morning light sneaking through my blinds catches on his fur.

I should be freaking out. Normal people would be freaking out, right? Instead, I'm sitting here, watching the steady rise and fall of his chest, remembering how it felt when he pulled me close last night. How his wings wrapped around us both like we were in our own private universe. How his voice got softer and softer as we talked about everything and nothing until the sky started turning pink.

"What are you doing to me?" I whisper, reaching out to trace the edge of his wing with my fingertip. The texture is impossibly soft, like touching a cloud made of silk. He makes this quiet chirping sound in his sleep that shoots straight to my heart.

This is crazy. All of it. I'm harboring a cryptid in my house, fucking said cryptid, falling for said–

No. Not going there. Not yet. But watching him sleep, seeing how vulnerable he looks despite being literally supernatural, I know I'm already in way too deep. The scariest part? I'm not sure I want to head back to the shallow end...

I drag myself through my morning routine, but my mind keeps drifting back to my bedroom. Every normal action feels absurd – how am I supposed to just go to work like everything's normal when there's Mothman in my bed? When there are men in black suits prowling around town looking for him?

My hands shake slightly as I button my uniform shirt. That car last night – three times it drove past my house. Once is nothing. Twice is coincidence. Three times? That's definitely surveillance. I've seen enough movies to know how this goes.

I pause in front of my mirror, trying to smooth down my hair and look like someone who definitely isn't hiding anything suspicious. The dark circles under my eyes aren't helping.

"This is fine," I mutter to my reflection. "Totally fine. I'll just go to work, act normal, and come straight home." But the knot in my stomach tightens as I remember those men at the hotel. Their perfectly pressed suits. Their calculated movements. The way they looked at my name tag.

Maybe I should call in sick? But that would probably look more suspicious. Besides, I need this job – supernatural house-guests don't pay the bills.

A soft rustling sound makes me jump, and I turn to find Thrax's eyes glowing dimly in the semi-darkness of my bedroom. Even half-asleep, those red orbs make my breath catch. It's like looking at twin blood moons.

"You are anxious," he says, his voice that impossible mixture of chirp and whisper that I'm starting to find devastatingly endearing. He sits up and tilts his head in that bird-like way of his. "I can feel it radiating off you."

"Oh, can you now?" I try for sarcasm, but my voice wavers. "Sorry if my completely rational fear of government agents breaking down my door is disturbing your beauty sleep."

He laughs in that melodic chitter of his. "Sarah..." It's just my name, but the way he says it makes my knees weak. "Come here."

I perch on the edge of the bed, and he immediately wraps one wing around my shoulders. The injured one stays carefully folded against his back.

"They could hurt you," I whisper. "You're already injured and unable to fly. If they come while I'm gone-"

"I have evaded humans for longer than you have been alive," he interrupts, a hint of amusement in his voice. "Even with an injured wing, I am far from helpless." His free wing flexes, displaying an impressive span that somehow manages to look both beautiful and menacing in my small bedroom.

"But-"

"I can sense them coming from miles away," he continues, pulling me closer. "Their fear, their determination, their purpose – it all has a distinct flavor. And I am very good at disappearing when I need to."

I want to believe him. The quiet confidence in his voice is reassuring, but... "What if they have special equipment? What if-"

He presses what passes for his forehead against mine, effectively silencing me. "Go to work, Sarah. I will be here when you return." There's a promise in those words that makes my heart flutter, even as my brain continues to spin worst-case scenarios.

"You're impossible," I mutter, but I can feel some of my anxiety ebbing away despite myself.

"So I have been told," he replies, and I swear I can hear him smiling.

I lean in to give him a quick goodbye peck – something casual, something that won't make me even later for work than I already am. But as I get close, his arms tighten around me, and suddenly I'm being pulled onto the bed with a surprised squeak.

"Hey!" I protest, although admittedly I am laughing too. "I have to go to work!"

"In a minute," he murmurs, and then he's kissing me. It's still strange – his face isn't exactly made for kissing in any human sense – but we've figured out our own way. The soft brush of his mandibles press against my lips, sending electricity down my spine. His wings create this perfect little world where nothing exists except us, the warmth of his body against mine, and the way my heart is trying to beat its way out of my chest.

When he finally releases me, I'm breathless and definitely going to be late for work. "That," I manage to say, "was not playing fair."

He makes that chittering laugh again. "Who said anything about playing fair?"

I scramble off the bed, trying to straighten my now-rumpled uniform. "Just... stay safe, okay?"

"Always," he promises.

Chapter Fourteen

My hands tremble as I refill the coffee urns, my attention split between this mundane task and the three men in identical black suits who materialized in the hotel lobby an hour ago.

One of them is speaking with a colleague of mine at the front desk. Another stands near the breakfast room, pretending to be absorbed in his phone but glancing up every few seconds to survey the room. The third moves between guests with practiced ease, engaging in what appears to be casual conversation.

I'm halfway through restocking napkins at the coffee station when one of them approaches. I know he's there before I turn around – something about the way the air changes, like a storm front moving in.

"Miss Walker." His voice is precise, measured. I turn to find him smiling at me, but it's an empty smile that doesn't reach his eyes. "Agent Miller. Do you have a moment?"

My heart stumbles, but I manage what I hope is a normal smile. "Of course. How can I help you?"

"Just a few routine questions." He produces a small notebook, and I notice his hands are perfectly steady. Too steady, like he's practiced this exact movement hundreds of times. "How long have you worked at the Point Pleasant Hotel?"

"Three years this October." I fold a napkin absently, just to give my hands something to do.

"And you live locally?"

"Yes." The word comes out a bit too quickly. I force myself to slow down. "About fifteen minutes from here." He makes a note, though I can't imagine what's noteworthy about that.

"Do you typically work the night shift, or the day shift?"

My stomach clenches. Why is he asking about my shifts? Are they tracking my movements? "I rotate shifts. Mostly mornings lately."

"Interesting." He glances at his notebook. "Several witnesses reported unusual activity in the McClintic Wildlife Management Area. Would you know anything about that?"

I think of that night, of Steve's panicked face, of wings blocking out the stars.

"The wildlife area?" I try to laugh, but it sounds hollow. "I avoid that place after dark. Too many teenagers drinking and telling urban legends."

His pen stops moving. "Urban legends?"

Fuck. Why did I say that?!

"You know, Mothman sightings. There's been this whole trend lately with the convention in town." I'm babbling now, my words coming too fast. "People in costumes, playing pranks-"

"Miss Walker." His interruption is soft but cuts like a knife. "We're investigating a missing person's case. These sightings coincide with the disappearance." He takes a step closer, lowering his voice. "Sometimes civilians notice things without realizing their significance. Even small details could be crucial."

I think of wings, of red eyes, of trust given and promises made. Of the way he curled into my blankets this morning, vulnerable and perfect.

"No," I say, my voice steadier than I feel. "Nothing unusual."

He studies me for a long moment, and I fight the urge to look away. His eyes are an unsettling shade of gray.

"Are you certain? Because we have reports of unusual activity near your street last night."

Shit, so it was the MIB in the car last night.

"Like I said, I've not seen anything unusual. On my street or otherwise."

"Thank you," His tone suggests he doesn't believe me for a second. He closes his notebook with a soft snap that makes me flinch. "If you do notice anything peculiar, we'll be around. Here's my card."

I take it automatically, the crisp white cardstock feeling like it's burning my fingers. There's no agency listed, just his name and a phone number.

"Thank you for your time, Miss Walker." He turns to leave, then pauses. "Oh, and Sarah?" The use of my first name sends ice down my spine. "Be careful on your way home tonight. There have been some incidents in the area regarding poor drivers. It would be tragic if anything were to happen to you."

The threat is so perfectly wrapped in concern that for a moment, I almost miss it. By the time I think to respond, he's already walking away, leaving me clutching his card and wondering if I've just made a terrible mistake by lying to the government. But worse than that is the certainty that he knows – maybe not everything, but enough.

I think of Thrax at home, sleeping peacefully in his nest of blankets, completely unaware of the danger. They already know my street. They probably know which house is mine. They're probably on their way there right now.

I need to get home. Now.

I grab my phone and type out a quick message to my manager: "Family emergency. Need to leave early." I don't wait for a response. Let them give me a warning. Let them fire me. I don't care. The only thing I care about is Mothman.

Chapter Fifteen

My hands are shaking so badly I drop my keys twice before managing to unlock the front door. The sound of them clattering against the porch makes me flinch. Everything seems too loud, too conspicuous. Like there might be eyes watching from every shadow, marking down my suspicious behavior in neat little notebooks with government-issue pens.

The house is quiet when I step inside. That weird kind of quiet that makes your ears ring, like the silence itself is trying to tell you something. I press my back against the door after I close it, letting out a breath. My legs are wobbly, the adrenaline crash hitting me all at once.

"Just breathe," I whisper to myself, but my voice sounds wrong in the stillness. Too high, too thin. "Everything's fine. You're fine."

The lie tastes bitter on my tongue.

I make my way to the bedroom where I left Mothman this morning. The door's cracked open just enough for me to peer inside. The afternoon sun paints golden stripes across the floor through the blinds, and there he is – curled up on his nest of blankets, wings tucked close. His chest rises and falls in that unique rhythm I've come to know so well.

For a moment, watching him sleep, I can almost pretend everything's normal. That we're just two people (well, one person and one cryptid) figuring out this crazy thing between us. But then I remember the MIB's cold eyes, the way he said "unusual activity" like he was reading from a script designed to make my skin crawl. The weight of what we're facing settles back onto my shoulders, heavier than before.

I slide down the wall next to the door, drawing my knees to my chest. God, what are we going to do?

The question echoes in my head as I watch him sleep, and suddenly the answer hits me with the force of a freight train. We can't keep doing this. Playing house, pretending the outside world doesn't exist. Those men in black aren't going to give up, and my little suburban home isn't exactly a fortress. Sooner or later, they'll find him. And then...

My throat tightens at the thought of what they might do to him. The tests, the experiments. The way they'd treat him like a specimen instead of someone who makes adorably confused faces when watching reality TV.

He needs to go back. Back to the inner-earth. The thought makes my heart feel like it's being squeezed in a vice, but I know it's right. It's the only way to keep him safe.

But how? It's not like there's a guidebook for sending your cryptid boyfriend back to his dimension.

I run my fingers through my hair, tugging in frustration. I don't know the first thing about interdimensional travel or secret underground realms or-

Wait.

Steve. Weird, enthusiastic, conspiracy-theory Steve. The only person I know who's as obsessed with Mothman as me.

I push off the wall, my decision made, and sneak into the bedroom. The moment I step inside, I'm reminded of the chaos I left behind this morning – yesterday's work uniform tossed over a chair, an empty coffee mug on the nightstand, and, most importantly, the overflowing laundry hamper in the corner.

I crouch in front of it, wrinkling my nose at the mix of yesterday's clothes and whatever I threw in there last week. My hands sift through the pile, moving socks and shirts aside until I spot them: my trousers from the other day. The ones with the crumpled business card that I stuffed in the pocket.

I grab them, shaking out the wrinkles, and shove my hand into the pocket. There it is. The business card is slightly damp from its time in the hamper, but Steve's phone number and email are still legible.

For a moment, I just stare at it. My stomach churns, and I clutch the card tighter, my mind spinning with worst-case scenarios. If I call him, I'll have to explain I've been harboring Mothman. He'll definitely have questions about the *physical* side of things.

The thought makes my cheeks burn. How do you even begin a conversation like that?

Hi, remember me? The girl who bailed on your cryptid-themed hookup? Well, funny story – I'm currently harboring the real Mothman. Oh, and we're fucking. I'm pretty sure I'm falling in love.

Steve could laugh. Or he could freak out. He could think I've completely lost it and call the men in white coats. Or worse – he could call the government.

I press my fingers to my temples, willing the anxiety to quiet down. None of that matters right now. I can't do this alone, and Steve is the only person who might actually be able to help.

I smooth out the card, staring at the number like it's a lifeline. My hand shakes as I pull out my phone and start typing it in, each digit feeling heavier than the last. When I finish, I hesitate one last time, my thumb hovering over the call button.

"You can do this," I whisper to myself. "For him. For both of you."

I take a deep breath and press the button.

Chapter Sixteen

The first hint that evening is settling in comes with the faint glow of twilight filtering through the curtains, painting the living room in muted purples and greys. I sit on the couch, arms wrapped around my knees, staring blankly at the darkening sky. My thoughts are a tangled mess, looping endlessly between the danger we're in and the impossible choices ahead.

A soft rustling sound pulls me from my spiral. I glance over to see Mothman stepping into the room, his wings shifting slightly as he adjusts to the space. The dim light catches on his glossy fur. He tilts his head, those glowing red eyes locking onto me with immediate focus.

"You are upset," he says, his voice carrying that strange mix of chirp and whisper. It's not a question.

I let out a shaky breath, pressing my fingers against my temples. "Yeah. You could say that."

He steps closer, his movements fluid but cautious, like he's not sure if he's intruding. His wings twitch, a subtle indication of his concern.

"Sarah, what is wrong?" he asks, lowering himself onto the chair across from me, his gaze never leaving mine.

I hesitate, my hands gripping the edge of the couch cushion like it might anchor me against the tide of emotions rising in my chest.

"We need to talk," I say finally, my voice low and uneven.

Thrax's head tilts slightly, his wings giving another small twitch. He moves from the arm of the chair to sit beside me on the couch.

"What is it?" he asks, his tone soft but laced with unease.

I glance down at my hands, struggling to find the right words.

"It's not safe for you here," I start, my heart tightening as his wings shift. "The men in black suits, the cars driving past the house, people asking questions at work... It's only going to get worse. They're looking for you."

He doesn't say anything, but I can feel his eyes on me, sharp and searching. I push forward, the words tumbling out now.

"You don't belong here, not in this world. If they find you, I don't even want to imagine what they'll do. Experiments, cages... I can't let that happen to you. You need to go back to the inner-earth. It's the only way you'll be safe."

Mothman's wings sag slightly, and his expression – despite its insect-like contours – manages to convey something achingly human.

"Do you not want me here?" he asks quietly, the words cutting through me like a knife.

My throat tightens, and it takes me a moment to respond.

"That's not it," I whisper, shaking my head. "It's not about wanting. It's about keeping you safe."

He shifts closer, his gaze piercing.

"Sarah, if your feelings have changed, I implore you to be honest with me."

The lump in my throat grows unbearable, and I bury my face in my hands for a moment, forcing myself to be honest.

"All I ever wanted was to meet you," I say, my voice breaking. "To see you, to know you. And these last few days... They've been incredible, like nothing I ever imagined. If it were up to me, this would never end." I look up at him, my eyes burning. "But it's not up to me. This world – it's dangerous for you. Every moment you're here is a risk, and I can't protect you from that."

For a moment, we just sit there, the silence stretching between us. Mothman's wings shift slightly, his glowing eyes dimming as he exhales a soft chitter that sounds almost like a sigh.

"If this is what you believe is best," he says, the weight in his tone unmistakable. "I will go."

I feel a pang of guilt at his reluctance, but I know this is the only way to keep him safe.

"I reached out to someone," I say carefully, gauging his reaction. "Someone who knows more about the inner-earth than I do."

His head tilts, curiosity momentarily flickering through his sadness. "Who?"

"Steve," I admit, managing a small, apologetic smile. "You remember, the guy who was with me the first night at the wildlife area? It turns out he knows a lot about conspiracy theories and inner-earth folklore. He thinks our best bet is to get you to Devil Horn Cave."

Mothman's brow furrows and his wings twitch. "Devil Horn Cave?"

"It's about a three-hour drive from here," I explain, "Steve thinks there's an opening to the inner-earth through the cave. If there's any chance of finding a way back for you, it's there."

He's quiet for a moment, his gaze shifting toward the darkened window. "And you trust this Steve?"

"I don't know who to trust," I reply honestly. "But right now, we need all the help we can get."

Mothman looks at me, his expression unreadable. "When do we leave?"

"Tomorrow morning," I say, my voice firm. "At dawn. The roads will be quieter, and it'll give us a chance to get there before anyone starts asking questions."

He nods, though his hesitation is clear.

"Sarah..."

"Yes."

"I love you."

Chapter Seventeen

Before I can second-guess myself, I close the distance between us. My hands tremble as I reach out to touch his chest, feeling the firmness of his muscles beneath. His skin is scorching hot under my fingertips and I can feel the rapid beating of his heart.

I trace the contours of his chest, mesmerized by the way his muscles ripple beneath my touch. A low growl rumbles in his throat as he's about to speak.

"Sssh," I say gently. "Don't say anything. My heart will break."

I take his hand in mind, and he stands. Silently, I lead him to the bedroom. His wings unfurl as we enter the room, casting shadows across the walls. I guide him to the bed, my legs trembling as I sit on the edge. He towers over me, red eyes burning.

Slowly, I reach out to caress his thighs, marveling at the raw power I feel beneath my fingertips. His muscles tense at my touch. I lean forward, pressing my lips to his abdomen. A shuddering breath escapes him as I trail kisses over his skin.

With gentle pressure, Thrax's strong hands push me backward onto the bed. My heart races as he kneels on the floor between my legs, his massive wings folding behind him. His glowing eyes roam over my body hungrily.

I prop myself up on my elbows, breath catching as he runs his hands up my thighs. He hooks his fingers under the waistband of my trousers, looking up at me questioningly. I nod, lifting my hips to help as he slowly slides them down my legs.

Cool air hits my exposed flesh, making me shiver. But then his hot breath is there, so close to where I ache for him. I let out a soft whimper of anticipation. His wings twitch and ruffle, betraying his own eagerness.

I can't contain the moan that escapes as his fingers brush against my inner thighs. His touch is impossibly gentle for such a powerful being. He traces feather-light patterns on my sensitive skin, slowly working his way higher.

My hips buck involuntarily as he finally reaches my aching center. His fingers ghost over my folds, barely making contact. I whimper, desperate for more pressure. As if reading my mind, he increases the firmness of his touch.

Thrax's large hand cups my mound, a finger sliding between my slick folds. I gasp at the sensation as he explores me intimately, mapping every curve and crevice. His thumb finds my swollen clit, circling it with maddening slowness.

"Please," I breathe, not even sure what I'm asking for.

Thrax responds to my plea, increasing the pressure and speed. His skilled fingers work me into a frenzy, stoking the fire building low in my belly. I writhe beneath his touch, grinding shamelessly against his hand.

Suddenly, I feel the warm wetness of his tongue joining his fingers. I cry out at the sensation, arching my back. His wings rustle and spread wide as he devours me hungrily.

I tangle my fingers in his soft downy fuzz, tugging gently. A rumbling growl vibrates against my core in response. The dual sensations of his tongue lapping at my sensitive flesh and the vibrations of his inhuman vocalizations quickly push me to the brink.

"Oh god, I'm so close," I pant, my thighs trembling as they clench around Thrax's head.

His glowing red eyes lock onto mine, filled with primal hunger. The intensity of his gaze sends me spiraling over the edge. Waves of pleasure crash over me as I come undone beneath him. My back arches off the bed, a keening cry escaping my lips. But Thrax doesn't let up, his skilled tongue working me through every aftershock.

As the last tremors subside, he comes to lie with me on the bed. I turn and gaze at him, breathless and flushed.

It's in this moment that I realize I love him. I love him and he's leaving tomorrow. And there is nothing I can do about it.

Chapter Eighteen

The highway stretches ahead like a dark ribbon, empty except for us. Trees crowd against both sides of the road, their branches reaching over the pavement like grasping fingers. I should feel relieved — we're actually doing this, getting him somewhere safe – but my hands are tight on the steering wheel, and I keep checking the rearview mirror every few seconds.

Thrax sits in the back of the car so he has more space and can duck down if needed. The sound of the engine seems too loud in the pre-dawn quiet. Even the radio feels wrong, so I've left it off. There's just the hum of tires on asphalt and the occasional rustle of his wings.

I glance in the rearview mirror and see something.

Shit.

A pair of headlights appear in my mirror, far behind us. It could be just another car, nothing to worry about. But something inside me tells me to be vigilant. I ease off the gas, watching. The car slows too. I speed up slightly, and there it is again. My mouth goes dry.

"Sarah?" Thrax's voice is soft, concerned. "What is wrong?"

I gesture toward the rearview mirror with a slight tilt of my head. "That black car. It's been following our every move for the last few minutes."

His wings twitch. He watches the mirror for a long moment, then says quietly, "They are following us."

A chill runs down my spine as I press down harder on the gas pedal.

The black sedan surges forward suddenly, eating up the distance between us. My heart slams against my ribs as the headlights flood my mirrors, turning everything behind us into harsh white light. The quiet tension of moments ago explodes into full-blown panic.

"I can feel them," Thrax says, his voice tight. His wings are pressed flat against the seat now, this antenna rigid. "Their fear and their determination. Like a blade aimed straight at us. They want me, Sarah. I can sense it."

I don't answer – can't answer – because we've hit the mountain roads and every ounce of concentration I have is focused on handling the curves. The steering wheel fights against my grip as we weave through switchbacks, the tires humming against the asphalt. But the black car stays with us, matching every turn, every acceleration. Their headlights are a constant presence in my mirrors, so bright they're leaving spots in my vision.

"Hold on!" I shout as we approach a particularly nasty curve. The sign says 20 mph, but we're doing at least fifty. I try to brake, but we're carrying too much speed. The car lurches sideways, and for one heart-stopping moment, I'm sure we're going into the ditch. Thrax's claws dig into the passenger seat in front of him as I wrench the wheel, somehow keeping us on the road.

In my mirror, I catch a glimpse of the black car fishtailing through the same curve. They recover quickly – too quickly – and surge forward again, their engine roaring in the night. These aren't amateur drivers behind us. They know exactly what they're doing.

Through the glare of headlights and the blur of adrenaline, I spot salvation: a gas station sign glowing in the darkness ahead. Without signaling – because who signals when they're being chased by government agents – I wrench the wheel hard, tires screaming as we careen into the lot.

"Get down," I hiss at Thrax, already reaching for my wallet. "Try to fold your wings as tight as you can. Make yourself small, and hide under the blankets." He nods and somehow manages to squeeze himself down onto the backseat. It's not perfect, but it'll have to do.

I step out, trying to keep my movements casual as I start pumping gas. My hands are shaking so badly I almost drop my credit card.

Just a normal person getting gas. Nothing to see here. Definitely no cryptids in the backseat.

The black car pulls in smoothly, parking near the store entrance. Three figures emerge – two men and a woman, all in identical black suits despite the early hour. They move with an unnervingly coordinated precision. The woman and one of the men head into the store, while the other lingers by the pump opposite mine, pretending to check his phone. But I can feel his gaze sweeping over my car, methodical and searching.

I glance toward the store. Through the fluorescent-lit windows, I can see the other agents pretending to browse, but their attention is focused entirely on me. I need to do something, and fast.

I finish pumping gas and open the car door, pretending to look for something.

"Stay down," I murmur. "I'll be right back."

I head in to pay for the gas but I notice all three agents in the store now. And they're casually blocking the exit. My mind races, wondering how to get past them.

That's when I spot it – a towering display of potato chips near the counter. Without letting myself think too hard about it, I stumble, catching my hip against the display. The bags cascade down in a noisy avalanche of foil and air.

"Oh my god, I'm so sorry!" I exclaim, loud enough to draw everyone's attention. While the clerk rushes over and the agents instinctively turn to look, I slip backward toward the door, my car keys already in hand. By the time they realize what's happening, I'm already sliding behind the wheel, my heart thundering in my chest as I turn the key.

The engine roars to life, but my brief moment of triumph dies instantly – the black sedan is already moving, cutting off our escape route. There must have been a fourth agent in the car still.

They've boxed us in, the nose of their car blocking the exit. I freeze, hands white-knuckled on the wheel.

"There!" Thrax's voice is urgent from the back seat. "Between the building and the dumpster."

I don't hesitate. The car lurches forward as I slam on the gas, aiming for the gap he pointed out. It's a tight squeeze – so tight I can hear the horrible scrape of metal against the dumpster's edge. But we make it through, bursting out onto what looks like a service road behind the station.

The gravel surface catches me off guard. My sedan wasn't built for this, and every rock that pings against the undercarriage makes me wince. In the rearview mirror, I see Thrax gripping the doorframe, his wings trembling with each bounce and jolt. The black car is already behind us again, their heavier vehicle handling the rough terrain much better than mine.

Up ahead, I see a dirt path cutting into the woods. It's barely wide enough for a car, more like maintenance access than a real road, but right now it's our only option. I wrench the wheel hard, and we plunge into the darkness between the trees.

Branches scrape against the windows like desperate fingers. The path is so narrow that patches of undergrowth catch beneath the car, creating a horrible dragging sound. But when I dare to glance in the mirror, I see the black sedan struggling to follow. They're too wide for this trail, their fancy car getting scratched to hell by the close-pressing trees.

"There!" Thrax points to an overgrown side path, almost invisible. I turn sharply, guiding us into the thick vegetation, then kill the engine and the lights. We sit in complete darkness, hardly daring to breathe. A moment later, the black sedan roars past our hiding spot, its headlights sweeping through the trees but missing us entirely.

We wait, frozen, until the sound of their engine fades into the distance. Only then do I let out the breath I've been holding, my hands finally loosening their death grip on the steering wheel.

The forest is utterly silent around us, broken only by the ticking of the cooling engine and my ragged breathing. My hands won't stop shaking on the steering wheel, even though we're not moving anymore. The adrenaline crash is hitting me hard, making everything feel slightly unreal.

A touch on my shoulder makes me jump – but it's just Thrax, his clawed hand gentle as it rests there. The familiar weight of it anchors me, pulling me back from the edge of panic.

"Sarah..." he starts, but I shake my head.

"We're not stopping," I say, my voice stronger than I expected. "We're getting you home. Those people? They're exactly why you can't stay." I meet his gaze, finding my resolve in those otherworldly eyes. "I won't let them take you."

He nods once, his hand squeezing my shoulder gently before withdrawing. I take a deep breath, turn the key in the ignition, and guide us carefully back onto the main road. The first hints of dawn are starting to lighten the sky, and somewhere ahead lies Devil Horn Cave – and his way home.

We've come too far to turn back now.

Chapter Nineteen

The landscape becomes something alien as we approach Devil Horn Cave. The terrain shifts from soft forest floor to sharp, broken stone that seems to have been thrust upward by some violent geological tantrum. Massive boulders sit like forgotten monuments, their surfaces etched with lichen and deep, shadowy cracks. The trees thin out here, giving way to a landscape that feels more like the edge of something – the boundary between one world and another.

And there it is. The cave mouth looms ahead, a black wound in the mountainside. It's wider than I expected, ringed with jagged rocks that look like teeth. Nothing about this place feels welcoming. Everything feels like a warning.

Thrax moves ahead of me, his wings folded tight against his body. We're both moving quickly now, our earlier caution replaced by an urgent need to complete this journey. He glances back occasionally, not speaking, but each look carries the weight of everything we can't say.

We're close now. So close to the entrance that I can feel the first whispers of cold air emerging from its depths. Thrax pauses, and our eyes meet. No words. Just a look that says everything and nothing at all.

I step forward, but my feet feel like they're made of lead. The cave entrance yawns before us – dark, impossibly deep. Thrax is already half-turned toward it, but something in me can't move. Can't let go.

"I should say something profound," I manage, my voice sounding strange and thin. "But I don't think there are words for this."

He turns, those red eyes catching the morning light. There's something ancient in that gaze – a depth that goes beyond human understanding.

"You saved me," he says simply. His clawed hand reaches out, hesitates, and then touches my cheek. "When no one else would."

My chest feels like it's collapsing inward.

"It was you that saved me," I whisper. "I was lost before I met you. You changed everything about my world." The words sound inadequate, like trying to describe an ocean with a thimble.

He pulls me close. Not gently, exactly, but with a kind of profound care that transcends gentleness. When he kisses me, it's like being touched by something beyond human comprehension – part creature, part shadow, part impossible miracle.

For just a moment, everything else falls away. There's just us. Our love is the bridge between two impossible worlds.

A rustle in the trees alerts us that something is wrong. Thrax freezes, his entire body going rigid. His antennae twitch and his wings unfurl slightly.

"Sarah," he says. That's all. Just my name. But it's enough to tell me that I should run.

The trees explode with motion. Black-suited figures emerge from impossible angles – behind boulders, from between trees, as if they've been waiting, perfectly still, for hours. A weighted net comes flying toward Thrax, its edges weighted with something that gleams metallically in the light.

But he's already moving. Not running – fighting. His wings slice through the air, catching the net mid-flight and tearing it like tissue paper. Tranquilizer darts hiss past him, some embedding in trees, others skittering across the rocky ground.

I try to move, but hands grab me from behind. Gloved hands, strong and precise.

"No!" I scream, but it's lost in the chaos. Thrax is a blur of motion – those massive wings create shockwaves that push the agents backward.

Another net comes. Then another. He tears through them like they're nothing, his movements a dance of impossible violence and grace. But they keep coming. More agents. More nets. More darts. More guns.

A hand clamps over my mouth. Another restrains my arms. I'm being dragged backward, fighting every inch of the way.

"THRAX!"

The scream is muffled, desperate.

As they're shoving me into the van, I catch a glimpse of something miraculous. His wings are spread. Wider than I've ever seen them. More beautiful than I could have ever imagined. He rises up, the agents blown back by the immense power of his thrusts. Scattered like leaves in a hurricane. I've never seen him fly before. Never seen the full power of what he truly is.

He rises. Straight up. The agents scatter,, their nets and weapons suddenly useless against this impossible creature taking flight.

The last thing I see before they slam the van doors is his silhouette against the morning sky, wings spread, surrounded by fallen agents. Perfect, and impossibly free.

Chapter Twenty

The van jerks to a sudden stop, throwing me against the metal wall. My shoulder aches from the impact, but there's no time to dwell on it. The doors swing open, and cold air rushes in, stinging my skin. Before I can orient myself, rough hands grab me, dragging me out into the open.

"Move," one of them barks, shoving me forward.

I stumble, barely catching my footing on the uneven ground. A sack is shoved over my head, the coarse fabric scratching my face and plunging me into darkness. My breaths come faster, the musty smell of the sack closing in around me.

I try to focus on the sounds – the crunch of gravel underfoot, the low murmur of voices, the distant hum of machinery. My senses strain for any clue about where I am or what they're planning to do.

Their grip on my arms is firm, unrelenting, as they steer me through what feels like a doorway. The air shifts, colder now, with an antiseptic tang that turns my stomach. I can hear faint beeping, like monitors, and the echo of footsteps on tile.

I bite my lip, forcing myself to stay calm. Thrax is still out there. He's not going to let them take me without a fight.

But the weight of the straps around my wrists and the firm shove onto what feels like a hard table make it hard to hold on to that hope. The sack presses tighter as they lean over me, voices low and clinical.

Stay strong, Sarah. Stay strong.

The sack is yanked off my head with a rough tug, and I squint as harsh fluorescent lights burn into my eyes. The brightness feels like a physical assault after so long in darkness. I blink rapidly, trying to adjust.

When my vision clears, the reality of my situation slams into me. I'm strapped to a cold metal table, my wrists and ankles bound tightly with thick straps that bite into my skin. The air smells sterile – like bleach and something faintly chemical – while a low hum from nearby machines fills the silence.

The room is stark and clinical, walls lined with monitors that display indecipherable readings. A tray of syringes and surgical tools sits on a wheeled cart to my right. Great. I'm getting lo-botomized, aren't I?

By the door, a soldier stands rigid, his weapon slung across his chest. His face is expressionless, his eyes fixed straight ahead as if I don't even exist.

Two figures in white lab coats hover nearby, flipping through a tablet and murmuring to each other. Their voices are calm, detached. The way they glance at me – like I'm a particularly interesting specimen – sends a shiver down my spine.

"Fascinating," one of them says, his tone more suited to discussing a lab rat than a person. "The connection is stronger than anticipated. She could be the key to luring him in."

"Agreed," the other replies, adjusting her glasses. "The pheromonal response suggests a biological link. If we can isolate the markers…" Her voice trails off, her eyes narrowing as she looks at me over.

"What are you talking about?" I snap, my voice shaky but defiant.

The man glances at me, not with sympathy but with a clinical sort of interest. "You're quite the anomaly, Miss… Sarah, is it? Your interaction with the subject has provided us with invaluable insight."

"What interaction?" I demand, though we all know what interaction they mean.

The woman smirks. "Don't play coy. You and the creature bonded. That makes you uniquely important to our research."

The female scientist turns away, her back to me as she busies herself with something on the metal cart. The clink of glass and soft whirring sounds make my skin crawl with dread. I crane my neck, desperate to see what she's doing, but the straps hold me firmly in place.

When she turns back, my breath catches in my throat. In her gloved hand, she holds an impossibly long needle, its metallic surface gleaming under the harsh lights. The syringe attached to it is filled with a swirling, iridescent liquid.

"Please," I whisper, my voice cracking. "Don't do this. You don't understand what you're dealing with. He'll come for me. He'll come rescue me."

"That's what we're counting on," the male scientist replies with a cold smile. "Your connection to the creature is precisely what we need."

As the woman approaches with the syringe, panic claws at my throat. I thrash against the restraints, desperate to escape, but they hold fast. The soldier by the door doesn't even flinch.

"Hold still," the woman orders, her voice devoid of emotion. "This will only hurt for a moment, and then, I think you'll quite enjoy it..."

The needle pierces my skin, and I cry out as liquid fire courses through my veins. I arch against the restraints, a strangled cry escaping my lips as the sensation intensifies.

The scientists exchange knowing glances, their eyes gleaming with clinical fascination as they observe my reaction.

The burning sensation slowly recedes, replaced by an intense tingling that spreads through my entire body. My skin feels impossibly sensitive, every slight movement of air across it sending shivers down my spine. My breathing grows shallow and rapid as warmth blooms deep in my core, radiating outward.

A pulsing ache builds between my thighs, my hips shifting restlessly against the cold metal table. My nipples tighten painfully, straining against the fabric of my shirt. Every nerve ending feels electrified, hyper-aware.

Fuck. They've given me something to make me aroused. Those sick fucks are using my pheromones to attract Mothman!

The female scientist approaches again, her eyes glinting with clinical curiosity behind her glasses. Without a word, she grasps the hem of my t-shirt and slowly lifts it, exposing my midriff. The cool air of the lab makes my skin pebble with goosebumps. She continues upward, pushing the fabric over my breasts, bunching it just beneath my chin. Next, her latex-gloved fingers slide beneath the edge of my bra. With practiced efficiency, she yanks the cups down, exposing my breasts to the cool air.

I'm not sure what they were expecting here. Probably for me to protest, scream for them to stop. Lucky for them, I'm a freak...

The female scientist slides a hand over my breast, her gloved fingers pinching my nipple. My breath hitches as a wave of pleasure ripples through me.

"Fascinating," the male scientist murmurs, scribbling notes. "The subject's arousal levels are off the charts. This should produce a potent pheromone signature."

These scientists have no idea what they are dealing with. Mothman is coming, and when he does, they'll be in big trouble.

Speaking of coming... The female scientist has pulled my trousers and underwear down to where the straps of the table meet my ankles. And she appears to be holding a dildo. *Nice.*

The woman scientist smirks as she positions the dildo between my legs. "Let's see just how potent we can make it, shall we?"

As she slowly pushes the toy inside me, I cry out - partly in pleasure, partly in frustration.

"You're doing it all wrong, " I say.

The female scientist pauses, her eyebrow arching in surprise. "Excuse me?"

"You heard me," I pant, my hips shifting restlessly against the cold metal table. "If you want to really crank up the pheromones, you're going about it all wrong."

The male scientist leans in, his curiosity piqued. "Do tell, Miss Sarah. How would you suggest we proceed?"

I can't believe I'm about to give pointers on how to properly arouse me to lure in my cryptid lover, but here we are. "First off, that dildo? Way too small. Mothman's hung like a horse. You need something bigger. Much bigger."

The female scientist glances at her colleague, then back at me with a mixture of skepticism and intrigue. She reaches behind her to a shelf lined with an impressive array of sex toys. Her hand hovers over a dildo that looks more substantial than the first.

"Bigger," I insist, my voice husky with need. "Think less 'human' and more 'mythical creature.'"

She selects a larger toy, holding it up for my inspection. I shake my head, gesturing with my chin toward an absolutely monstrous dildo at the far end of the shelf. It's easily the size of my forearm, with ridges and bumps along its length that make my inner walls clench in anticipation.

The male scientist's eyebrows shoot up. "Surely you can't be serious. That would cause significant discomfort, if not injury."

I laugh, the sound breathy and tinged with desire. "Trust me, doc. When you're dealing with cryptid anatomy, you've got to think outside the box. Besides," I add with a wink, "I'm more flexible than I look."

The female scientist hesitates for a moment before grabbing the massive dildo. She approaches me slowly, her eyes darting between my face and my exposed pussy.

"You're sure about this?" she asks, a hint of uncertainty in her voice.

I nod eagerly, spreading my legs as wide as the restraints will allow.

The female scientist positions the massive dildo at my entrance, her eyes wide as she slowly pushes it inside. I gasp as the thick head stretches me, a delicious burn spreading through my core. Inch by glorious inch, she works it deeper, my inner walls clenching and fluttering around the intrusion.

"Oh god," I moan, my head thrown back against the table. "Yes, just like that!"

She pauses, giving me a moment to adjust before pressing onward. The ridges and bumps along its length send shockwaves of pleasure through me with each thrust. My hips buck against the restraints, desperate for more friction.

"More," I pant, arching my hips as much as the restraints allow. "Don't hold back."

She obliges, pushing the toy deeper. I cry out as it fills me impossibly full, the ridges along its length dragging against my sensitive walls. My body trembles, adjusting to the intense stretch.

"Oh fuck," I moan, my head falling back against the table. "That's it. Now move it."

The scientist begins to thrust the dildo, slowly at first, then picking up speed as my cries of pleasure grow louder. I strain against the restraints, desperate to grind my hips and take it deeper.

The female scientist's eyes widen as she watches me take the massive toy. She glances at her colleague, who's furiously scribbling notes.

"Remarkable," he mutters. "The subject's capacity for stimulation far exceeds our initial projections."

I laugh breathlessly. "You ain't seen nothing yet, doc. If you really want to crank up those pheromones, you're gonna need to work my clit too."

The woman hesitates, then reaches out with her free hand. Her latex-covered fingers find my swollen bud, circling it tentatively.

"Faster," I gasp.

She increases the pressure, her movements growing more confident as my moans of pleasure fill the room. The combination of her fingers on my clit and the massive dildo stretching me open has me climbing toward orgasm at an alarming rate.

Through half-lidded eyes, I watch the female scientist. Her cheeks are flushed, her breathing quickening as she works the toy inside me. There's a hunger in her gaze that goes beyond scientific curiosity.

"Oh god," I moan, my voice husky with need. "You're getting good at this."

The male scientist clears his throat. "Perhaps we should take a break to analyze the data," he suggests, his voice strained.

I seize the opportunity, locking eyes with the woman. "Actually," I purr, "I think we're just getting to the good part. But I can't cum if you're all looking at me."

The female scientist shrugs at her colleague.

"You heard her. She needs privacy."

The male scientist hesitates, his brow furrowed with uncertainty. But after a moment, he nods curtly and turns to leave. The soldier follows, closing the door behind them with a soft click.

Great. I've gotten rid of the guy with a gun, that will make things easier when Thrax arrives. But in the meantime...

The scientist leans in close, her breath hot against my ear.

"Now then," she purrs, her fingers trailing down my stomach. "Let's see just how potent we can make those pheromones, shall we?"

The scientist climbs up onto the table. She straddles my thigh, her heat evident even through the fabric of her trousers. With deft fingers, she unbuttons her lab coat and lets it slide off her shoulders.

Her hands roam over my body, teasing and exploring. She traces the curve of my breast, circling my nipple before giving it a sharp pinch that makes me gasp.

The scientist's eyes are dark with desire as she leans down, her breath hot against my skin.

"Let's see what all the fuss is about, shall we?" she murmurs, her voice husky with arousal.

The first swipe of her tongue along my slit has me crying out, my hips bucking against the restraints. She hums appreciatively, the vibration sending shivers through me.

"Mmm, you taste divine," she purrs.

Her tongue delves deeper, exploring every fold and crevice. My thighs tremble as she alternates between teasing licks and focused attention.

"Oh god," I moan, straining against the restraints. "Don't stop!"

Just as I'm on the brink of climax, a deafening crash shakes the room. The ceiling explodes inward in a shower of plaster and metal, sunlight streaming through the gaping hole. A dark shape descends, massive wings unfurling to fill the space.

The scientist jerks back, her eyes wide with terror as Thrax lands with earth-shaking force. His red eyes glow with otherworldly fury, muscles rippling beneath iridescent black fur. With lightning speed, one clawed hand shoots out, razor-sharp talons slicing across the scientist's throat.

A gurgling cry escapes her lips as crimson sprays from the wound. She stumbles back, hands clutching futilely at her neck, before collapsing to the floor. Her body twitches once, twice, then goes still, a pool of blood spreading beneath her.

"Thrax!" I cry out, relief and desire warring for dominance. "I knew you'd come! Get me out of these restraints!"

"It seems I'm not the only one who was coming," Thrax says with a low chuckle, his glowing red eyes roaming over my exposed body. "It seems you've been busy, Sarah."

"They were trying to use me as bait," I explain breathlessly, still trembling with need. "To lure you here."

Thrax's eyes narrow, a growl rumbling deep in his chest. "Then their plan worked. But I don't think they anticipated the consequences." His gaze falls on the fallen scientist, her lifeless eyes staring blankly at the ceiling. A twinge of guilt flashes through his eyes, but then it evaporates. "We need to untie you."

"Wait," I gasp, my mind racing. "The male scientist - he had the keys to these restraints on his belt. But he left the room."

Thrax's antennae twitch thoughtfully.

"No matter," he rumbles, his wings rustling with excitement. "I can release you another way."

Thrax's eyes gleam with predatory hunger as his massive form looms over me. I can feel the heat radiating from his body, smell his musky, alien scent. My pulse quickens as one clawed hand trails down my exposed torso.

"You are so beautiful like this," he purrs, voice deep and resonant. "All spread out and needy."

His other hand moves to the thick fur covering his groin. As I watch, transfixed, his cock emerges — that long, twisted amber flesh. It's even more magnificent than I remember.

Thrax wraps a clawed hand around his impressive length, stroking slowly. His red eyes burn into mine as he pleasures himself mere inches from me. I strain against the restraints, desperate to touch him, to taste him.

"Now? Really?!" I exclaim, equal parts aroused and exasperated. "We're in the middle of a secret government facility! Shouldn't we be escaping or something?"

"It won't take long," he purrs.

Thrax's hand moves faster along his length, the ridges and bumps catching the light. Pre-cum beads at the tip, glistening like liquid amber. My mouth waters at the sight. A bead drops, impossibly slow, onto the metal restraints. The metal fizzes and melts under its touch.

Of course! His acidic jizz! From the start of the story. Now, that's a good Chekhov's gun!

My eyes widen as I watch the metal restraint dissolve under the acidic drop. "Thrax, you're a genius! Quick, cum on these restraints!"

He grins, revealing rows of sharp teeth. "With pleasure."

Thrax's hand moves faster, his breathing growing ragged. I strain against the bonds, desperate to assist but unable to do more than offer encouragement.

"That's it," I urge, my voice husky. "Come on, big guy. Set me free."

Thrax's massive form tenses, his wings quivering as he nears his peak. But before we can finish, the male scientist stumbles in, his eyes widening in horror at the scene before him. Thrax, still panting and spasming, whirls to face the intruder.

"Dear god," the scientist chokes out, fumbling for the radio at his belt. "Security breach! The creature is here and trying to cum his way to freedom!"

Thrax roars in frustration, but his hand never leaves his throbbing cock, still stroking furiously.

"Don't stop!" I yell, kicking out with my partially freed leg as a soldier launches at us. My foot connects with his jaw, sending him sprawling.

More pour in through the door, their eyes wide with a mixture of horror and fascination at the scene before them. Thrax's massive form looms over me, his iridescent black fur rippling as he continues to pleasure himself.

I manage to wrench one arm free, the metal restraint half-dissolved by Thrax's pre-cum. I grab a nearby tray of medical instruments, hurling it at the approaching soldiers. Scalpels and forceps clatter across the floor, buying us precious seconds.

"Almost there," Thrax grunts, his massive body trembling with the effort.

The male scientist lunges forward, desperation in his eyes. "Stop! You don't understand what you're dealing with!"

I laugh, the sound edged with hysteria. "Oh, I understand perfectly. And I think you're about to get a very messy demonstration."

With a deafening roar, Thrax reaches his climax. Thick ropes of acidic cum arc through the air, splattering across my restraints. The metal hisses and bubbles, disintegrating rapidly.

Thrax whirls to face the soldiers and scientist, his massive cock still pulsing and twitching. With a guttural roar, he unleashes a torrent of spunk in their direction. The thick, creamy fluid shoots from his cock like a milky fireman's hose.

The first soldier screams as the viscous liquid splashes across his face and chest. His skin immediately begins to bubble and hiss, smoke rising from the points of contact. He claws desperately at his melting flesh, but it's futile. Within seconds, his features have dissolved into an unrecognizable mass of liquefying tissue.

The male scientist backpedals frantically, but he's not fast enough to escape the onslaught. A thick glob of Thrax's otherworldly seed splatters against his face. His screams join with those of the dissolving soldier. Their agonized cries echo through the sterile room as their bodies disintegrate before our very eyes.

Thrax's acidic cum has done its work, dissolving the last of my restraints. I leap off the table, my legs wobbly but determined. Thrax's massive arms wrap around me, pulling me close against his chest.

"Hold on tight," he rumbles, his wings unfurling with a thunderous whoosh.

I cling to him as he crouches, muscles coiling beneath me. With a powerful thrust of his legs, we launch upward through the gaping hole in the ceiling. The wind whips my hair wildly as we soar into the open sky, leaving behind the chaos and carnage of the secret facility.

Chapter Twenty-One

The afternoon sunlight blazes across the West Virginia mountains as we soar together. Well, I say together, but I'm basically holding on for dear life Thrax while he does all the work. Not exactly your standard romantic getaway.

"So," I call out over the rush of wind, "this is a fun couple activity – fleeing from government testing sites."

Thrax looks down at me briefly.

"So, we are a couple now, are we?"

I feel the heat crawl up my neck, grateful he can't see my face directly. "No, no. Of course not. Although, I don't usually have to dodge my friend's acidic cum. That feels like more of a friends-with-benefits thing."

He ignores my joke, pretending not to have heard me.

His wings catch a thermal, lifting us higher. Pine forests spread beneath us like a green carpet, rocky outcroppings jutting through like nature's own obstacle course. The mountains here are ancient and unapologetic, much like the creature carrying me.

I tighten my grip and try not to think about how good he feels against me. Complicated doesn't begin to cover what we have...

We land in a small clearing surrounded by towering pines. The ground is soft with decades of fallen needles, and the air feels thick with silence.

"You saved me," I say, the words feeling inadequate and obvious.

Thrax's hand hovers near mine. Not quite touching, but close enough that I can feel the heat radiating between us.

"I would destroy entire worlds before I'd let them take you," he says. The words should sound dramatic, but from him, they're just simple truth.

I laugh, but it's a watery sound. "That's the most romantic and terrifying thing anyone's ever said to me."

"Sarah," he continues, carefully, "I don't want to leave you. The government knows we have a connection, and I fear that even when I am gone, you will remain a target." He pauses, and a breeze rustles through the pines, carrying the scent of moss and secrets. "There may be another way."

"Another way for what?" I ask, though I'm not sure I want to know.

He looks away, a gesture so human it catches me off guard. When he speaks, his words come slowly, carefully measured.

"For us to be together," he says. "But it would mean leaving everything you know behind. Permanently."

The word hangs between us like a physical thing. Permanently. No going back. No family. No surface world. Just... us.

My heart pounds so loudly I'm certain he can hear it. The mountain breeze feels suddenly colder, the pine trees closing in like silent witnesses.

I take a deep breath. Look into those glowing red eyes that have haunted my dreams, saved my life, changed everything.

"Tell me," I say.

Chapter Twenty-Two

Every needle on every pine feels distinct. The moss-covered ground breathes beneath my feet. Each breath I take is a deliberate thing, parsed out like carefully counted currency. I'm acutely aware that this moment – right here, right now – is the last moment I'll exist as purely human.

The mountain clearing feels charged, electric. Sunlight filters through pine branches in fractured patterns, casting shadows that seem to move even when nothing's moving. My fingers trace idle patterns against my thigh, a nervous habit I've had since childhood.

Thrax approaches silently.

"Ready?" he asks, that single word holding entire universes of meaning.

I nod. Then pause.

"Will it hurt?"

"No," he says, his chittering undertone soft. I believe him.

My next question comes out small, vulnerable. "What if they find me? The government agents?"

His hand cups my cheek

"I will protect you," he says, and it sounds less like a promise and more like an immutable law of the universe. "I will not leave your side until it is done. No one will hurt you."

Another deep breath. The forest watches. I am ready.

I watch, transfixed, as silk begins to emerge from Thrax's wrists. It's nothing like I imagined – not the delicate threads from a silkworm, but something more substantial. Pearlescent and strong, with a slight iridescence that shifts between silver and pale blue. The silk moves with a strange intelligence, almost seeming to reach toward me of its own accord.

"Try not to move," he says.

The first threads wrap around my ankles, cool and impossibly smooth. They're stronger than steel cable but move like liquid. Each wrap is deliberate, calculated. Thrax's movements are methodical, almost surgical – no wasted motion, each thread placed with mathematical precision.

He lifts me with impossible ease, positioning me upside down beneath a thick pine branch. Gravity immediately becomes my enemy. Blood rushes to my head, creating a thunderous roar in my ears. The world tilts, spins, becomes a kaleidoscope of green and brown and filtered sunlight.

More silk. Wrapping. Binding. Not constraining, but transformative. Each layer feels like it's connecting to something beneath my skin. My body becomes a canvas, and he is the artist, creating something entirely new.

I'm dizzy. Disoriented. The forest spins around me, and I'm suspended – part of the landscape, yet separate. Waiting.

"Breathe," he says. "Just breathe."

Darkness first. Not black, but a darkness alive with possibility – shifting, breathing, pregnant with potential. Time becomes fluid, loses meaning. Am I seconds or centuries? My bones (are they still bones?) shift and meld and curl and itch. Something moves beneath my skin.

Fractured sensations bloom and dissolve. Fingers elongating, contracting, becoming something. Skin ripples like water, muscles rewriting their own blueprint. I am becoming and unbecoming. It's a language I do not yet understand.

Whispers. Not sound, but sensation. Memories that aren't memories. Fragments of something ancient, something that existed before human consciousness. Pine roots pulse with forgotten rhythms. The mountain's bones speak in frequencies beyond hearing.

Membranes thin as thought, strong as starlight. I am multiple things at once. I am not who I was. I am not what I was.

I am.

A crack. Light bleeds through silk threads. Another crack. Wider. Brightness erupts, sharp and clean and terrifying in its clarity.

I emerge.

Thrax's hands catch me. Slowly, the world comes into focus.

My first breath feels like a revelation. These lungs expand differently. Deeper. Fuller. The air tastes like pine and possibility.

I unfurl my wings experimentally. They're incredible – translucent at the edges, shimmering with an iridescence that catches the mountain light. When I move, they catch the sunlight like living stained glass.

"Holy shit," I mutter, twisting to get a better look. "I'm beautiful!"

Thrax watches, something like wonder in his glowing eyes.

"So," I say, a laugh bubbling up from somewhere deep and new, "I guess I'm not a Mothman. More of a... Mothma'am?"

He laughs and my heart swells with love.

I stretch my wings again, testing them. It feels natural, like I've always had them. Like they've been waiting inside me, dormant, just beneath my human skin.

Thrax steps closer, and when we kiss, it's like the mountain itself sighs.

Then we turn, together, towards the hidden cave that will lead us home.